## *"You and I both know this marriage doesn't stand a chance of lasting,"*

Sam said, his gaze narrowed.

"I didn't say I was interested in forever," Sarah returned, letting him know she had no intention of pemanently stripping him of his freedom. She moved toward him, her heart pounding. She'd never behaved so boldly before.

"Are you sure you know what you're doing?" Sam asked gruffly.

Sarah's jaw firmed with purpose. "I've been waiting a lot of years for Mr. Right to come along. He never has. If I wait any longer, I may never find out what all the shouting's about."

Shock replaced Sam's guardedness. "Are you saying you've never been with a man?"

"Never," Sarah admitted glumly.

Heat blazed in Sam's eyes. Sarah's heart beat so hard it was painful. She'd never been this nervous in her life.

Dear Reader,

This month we have a terrific lineup of stories, guaranteed to warm you on these last chilly days of winter. March comes in like a lion with a great new FABULOUS FATHER by Donna Clayton. Joshua Kingston may have learned a thing or two about child-rearing from his son's new nanny, Cassie Simmons. But now the handsome professor wants to teach Cassie a few things about love! The *Nanny and the Professor* is sure to touch your heart.

Elizabeth August concludes her WHERE THE HEART IS series with *A Husband for Sarah*. You've watched Sarah Orman in previous titles bring couples together. Now Sarah gets a romance—and a wedding—all her own!

A *Wife Most Unlikely* is what Laney Fulbright is to her best friend, Jack Austin. But Laney's the only woman this sexy bachelor wants! Linda Varner brings MR. RIGHT, INC. to a heartwarming conclusion.

Alaina Hawthorne brings us two people who strike a marriage bargain in *My Dearly Beloved*. Vivian Leiber tells an emotional story of a police officer and the woman he longs to love and protect in *Safety of His Arms*. And this month's debut author, Dana Lindsey, brings us a handsome, lonely widower and the single mom who's out to win his heart in *Julie's Garden*.

In the coming months, look for books by favorite authors Suzanne Carey, Marie Ferrarella, Diana Palmer and many others.

Happy reading!

Anne Canadeo
Senior Editor
Silhouette Romance

Please address questions and book requests to:
Silhouette Reader Service
U.S.: 3010 Walden Ave., P.O. Box 1325, Buffalo, NY 14269
Canadian: P.O. Box 609, Fort Erie, Ont. L2A 5X3

# ELIZABETH AUGUST

# A HUSBAND FOR SARAH

**Silhouette**
**R O M A N C E™**
Published by Silhouette Books
America's Publisher of Contemporary Romance

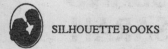

SILHOUETTE BOOKS

ISBN 0-373-19067-0

A HUSBAND FOR SARAH

This edition published by arrangement with Harlequin Enterprises B.V.

® and TM are trademarks of Harlequin Enterprises B. V., used under
license. Trademarks indicated with ® are registered in the United States
Patent and Trademark Office, the Canadian Trade Marks Office and in
other countries.

Printed in U.S.A.

**Books by Elizabeth August**

Silhouette Romance

*Author's Choice* #554
*Truck Driving Woman* #590
*Wild Horse Canyon* #626
*Something So Right* #668
*The Nesting Instinct* #719
*Joey's Father* #749
*Ready-made Family* #771
*The Man from Natchez* #790
*A Small Favor* #809
*The Cowboy and the Chauffeur* #833
*Like Father, Like Son* #857
*The Wife He Wanted* #881
*The Virgin Wife* #921
*Haunted Husband* #922
*Lucky Penny* #945
*A Wedding for Emily* #953
*The Seeker* #989
†*The Forgotten Husband* #1019
†*Ideal Dad* #1054
†*A Husband for Sarah* #1067

Silhouette Special Edition

*One Last Fling!* #871

*Smytheshire, Massachusetts Series
†Where The Heart Is

---

## ELIZABETH AUGUST

lives in western North Carolina with her husband, Doug, and her three boys, Douglas, Benjamin and Matthew. She began writing romances soon after Matthew was born. She has always wanted to write.

Elizabeth does counted cross-stitching to keep from eating at night. It doesn't always work. "I love to bowl, but I'm not very good. I keep my team's handicap high. I like hiking in the Shenandoahs, as long as we start up the mountain, so the return trip is down rather than vice versa." She loves to go to Cape Hatteras to watch the sun rise over the ocean.

Elizabeth August has also published books under the pseudonym Betsy Page.

# SARAH'S JALAPEÑO CORN BREAD

Preheat oven to 400° F. While oven is preheating and you are mixing the ingredients, place 10" cast-iron skillet in oven to heat. (Placing corn-bread batter in heated skillet gives it a more crusty outer coating.)

**Combine:**

2  cups stone-ground cornmeal
2  tsps baking powder
1  tsp baking soda
½ tsp salt

*Give dry ingredients a light stir to mix them, then add:*

1  slightly beaten egg
1  cup milk
1  8 oz can of pineapple tidbits from which the juice
   has been drained
1  cup grated cheddar cheese
⅛ to ¼ cup (depending on your taste) diced jalapeño
   peppers
   (handle peppers with care)
   *For a mild taste, be certain to remove all the seeds
    from the peppers. Or, you may try substituting
    green bell peppers.*

*Mix all ingredients until well-blended*

*Carefully* remove heated skillet from oven and add one tablespoon cooking oil (I prefer olive oil). With a spatula, spread oil around bottom of heated skillet. Next, pour batter into heated skillet. It will be thick, and you will have to spread it out until it is even. Return skillet to oven and cook for approximately 25 minutes or until corn bread is nicely browned.

# Chapter One

Sarah smiled with anticipation as she drove down the snow-covered road. Up ahead, she saw the break in the fence line and the big metal mailbox that marked her turnoff. In the back of her mind, she'd wondered if she'd recognize her destination after all this time. She had. In the distance, across the snow-covered landscape, she could see the sprawling ranch house where she'd spent so much of her youth. Smoke curled up from the chimney and a sense of homecoming she hadn't experienced in years swept through her.

As she slowed to make her turn, she noted that the several inches of snow that had fallen a few days ago had been cleared off the driveway. She guessed Sam Raven had done that. When she'd called to ask if she could come for a visit, her aunt had mentioned that Sam still worked for them.

"But I came anyway," she muttered, the thought of the man causing her nerves to tense. Immediately she grimaced at herself for still having such a strong re-action to him. It wasn't that she disliked Sam, she ad-mitted. He simply made her uneasy.

But he was a minor irritant. Again her jaw firmed. She had some unresolved business from her past that had to be settled. And that business revolved around Ward Anders.

A nervous tremor shook her as the image of a handsome blond-haired boy with deep blue eyes filled her mind. Silently she called herself a coward. She'd had to drive through Anders Butte to get to her aunt and uncle's ranch. Ward's family owned the only bank in the small town and, since his father's death, Ward had been president there. Originally she'd planned to stop and cash a check, just as an excuse to get a glimpse of him. But by the time she'd reached Anders Butte she'd changed her mind. Reminding herself that she wasn't a silly schoolgirl any longer, she'd driven on through town. When she was ready to face Ward, she'd march right up and say hello. There would be no ridiculous peeking around corners at him.

Besides, deep inside she'd felt an anxiousness to get to the ranch. The sense of homecoming increased as she turned onto the long driveway leading to the house. She hadn't expected to feel this strongly. The ranch had been in the Perry family for generations. She'd spent her summers here with her grandparents from the time she was barely nine years old. And, when her parents died when she was fourteen, she had come here to live with her grandparents.

But after her grandparents had both passed away, in spite of her aunt and uncle's encouragement for her to think of this place as her home, she'd found herself avoiding coming here. Most of her twenty year tenure as a navy nurse had been spent in San Diego, California, and she'd convinced Ruth and Orville to visit her in California every once in a while.

"I shouldn't have stayed away so long," she murmured under her breath as warm memories flooded her mind.

Nearing the house, she saw a plump gray-haired woman wearing a heavy sheepskin coat step out onto the front porch and wave.

The soft smile on Sarah's face broadened. She'd always been very fond of Ruth and Orville. Quickly, she parked, hopped out and hurried up the porch steps.

"Girl, you're a sight for sore eyes," Ruth said, greeting her with a tight hug. As she released her, her gaze turned to the vehicle in which Sarah had arrived. "That's one fancy truck you're driving," she remarked with an admiring smile.

Sarah turned to look at her new, red, heavy-duty pickup and grinned with pride. It had all the extras—an extended cab, four-wheel drive and a white camper top covering the loading bed. As a bonus, it had proven even more useful than she'd anticipated. Again she hoped the instincts that had brought her back to her childhood home were as good as those that had guided her to make this purchase. "The salesman back in San Diego thought it'd be too much machine for me to handle," she said. "But I told him he'd never been to the wilds of Wyoming in January." Sarah's grin became a little lopsided. "The truth is I'd been planning to buy a small four-wheel drive car of some sort. Then I saw this truck on the lot. I've always wanted a pickup and I'm not getting any younger."

Ruth shook her head. "Why you just turned forty-one your last birthday. By my reckoning you're still a young whippersnapper."

Sarah considered mentioning that she'd noticed a few gray strands mingled among the black ones this morning when she'd brushed and loosely plaited her hair into the single braid that hung halfway down her back. Then she reminded herself that her complexion was still young looking and there was still a spark in her gray eyes. "I don't think I qualify as a whippersnapper any longer," she said. "However, I'll admit I've got a few good years left."

"More than a few," Ruth stated firmly.

Sarah's attention had returned to her aunt. After all the years she'd spent as a nurse, she'd learned to recognize anxiousness even when a person was trying to hide it. "Something's wrong," she said bluntly. "Is it Uncle Orville? Is he ill?"

"Just had a touch of the flu but it's gone now," a man's voice said from the doorway.

Sarah turned to see her uncle. At seventy-five, his shoulders weren't quite as broad as they had been, but there was still an air of strength and authoritative bearing about him. However, the nurse in her was quick to note the paleness of his skin. And the easy way he leaned against the doorjamb, she guessed, was more because he was feeling dizzy than because he was relaxed.

"It's not gone and you should be in bed," Ruth declared, confirming Sarah's suspicions.

"I haven't got time to be sick. Now that Sarah's here to keep you company, I'm going looking for Sam," he announced, straightening himself away from the doorjamb.

Ruth's jaw firmed. "I'm sure Sam is just fine. He's been gone longer than this many times. And, he knows how to take care of himself."

Orville staggered slightly and Sarah rushed to his side, slipping an arm around his waist to steady him. "You're in no condition to go looking for anyone," she said sternly.

Orville tried to straighten and Sarah felt him wobble. With a resigned sigh, he slipped his arm over her shoulder and, using her as a crutch, allowed himself to be helped back to his bedroom. "If we haven't heard from him in an hour, I'm going to call the sheriff," he said as Sarah eased him into a sitting position on his bed.

"As soon as I get you back into bed, I'll call the sheriff," Ruth replied. She turned her attention to Sarah. "I'll take care of this cantankerous old man. You go get your suitcases. I've got your old room all ready for you."

"Cantankerous old man!" Sarah heard Orville protesting gruffly as she started toward the door.

Out of the corner of her eye, she saw Ruth shaking her head at her husband. "I call them as I see them," Ruth returned. But behind the stern expression on her face there was a tenderness that spoke of a lifetime of love.

A flash of envy swept through Sarah. She'd hoped to find that kind of love herself but never had. Then the moment of envy was gone. In its place was the image of Sam Raven as she'd last seen him. He stood six feet two inches and was strongly built. His heritage, a mixture of Cheyenne and Shoshone, was clearly evident in his features. He'd usually worn his long, thick black hair held in place by a leather thong tied across his forehead, except during roundups or when he was breaking a horse. Then he wove it into a single braid that hung down the center of his back. Sarah had always labeled that his "getting down to serious business" style.

In a way that had been a joke. Sam was never frivolous; not that she'd ever seen. He was only a couple of years older than she was, but he acted as if he was ancient and she was a mere child. His Indian name was Rumbling Thunder and, she'd always thought, it fit him perfectly.

"And if there's a man who could take care of himself, it's Sam Raven," she assured herself as she continued to her truck. Still, the uneasiness that had begun to build within her was fast turning to anxiousness.

Returning to the house with her suitcases, she stopped in the hall and listened while Ruth talked to the sheriff on the phone. The look on her aunt's face only caused her anxiousness to increase. "Something wrong?" she asked as Ruth hung up.

"There's been a bad accident. The sheriff's got every man he could deputize at the scene. It'll probably be dark before they can rescue all the victims. And, the only helicopter that's available will be needed to transport the worst injured to the hospital." Ruth raked a hand through her hair as she paced to the window and looked out.

"We can't afford to keep another full-time hand besides Sam on the payroll. In the winter, it's just Sam and Orville who take care of this place," she continued worriedly. Her jaw firmed. "I'm sure Sam's all right. Pauline Roundtree, the dispatcher in the sheriff's office, has known Sam all his life. She says he'll be fine. She says his grandfather knew the spirit of a snow wolf and taught Sam all that was needed to survive in the winter. And, like I reminded your uncle, it isn't unusual for Sam to be gone so long."

Sarah had the feeling these last reassuring statements were more an effort for Ruth to convince herself of Sam's well-being than for Sarah's ears. Joining her aunt at the window, she frowned up at the sky. "The weatherman was predicting more snow tonight."

Suppressed anger suddenly showed on Ruth's face. "If he'd remembered to take his walkie-talkie then we wouldn't have to be standing here worrying." She snorted. "Men! They always think they're invincible."

Sarah saw the increased anxiousness her aunt was trying to mask with anger, and her own uneasiness grew stronger. "How long has Sam been gone?"

Ruth's gaze again turned to the frigid landscape outside and her jaw trembled slightly. "Two and a half days. Some cows got out during the last snowfall. He went after them. Said that as long as he was going, he might as well check the fence line toward the north boundary."

An old memory stirred within Sarah. It was one she'd worked hard to bury and she shoved all but the location into the recesses of her mind. "There used to be a line shack in that direction," she said stiffly.

"It's still there."

"He can sit out the storm there."

Ruth nodded. "That's where I'm hoping he is. The roof's sturdy and Sam always sees that there's firewood there and a few tins of food."

Sarah glanced at her watch. "I figure there's four hours of daylight left," she said. "If I leave now, I can be at the shack before nightfall. If he did get himself injured and couldn't get back here, that'd be where he'd head."

Ruth gripped her arm. "You can't go out there."

"I know this ranch like the back of my hand," Sarah assured her. "And I haven't let myself get soft since I retired from the navy."

"I don't want to have to be worrying about both you and Sam," Ruth argued, continuing to hold on to Sarah's arm.

Resolve etched itself into Sarah's features. Loosening her aunt's grip by taking Ruth's hand in hers and giving it a loving squeeze, she said, "I'll be fine. I'm going to go." She wasn't certain why she felt so strong a desire to rescue Sam if he did need rescuing, but she did know she couldn't make herself sit around this house and wait. Already the walls felt as if they were closing in on her.

Ruth hesitated for a moment longer, then her composure broke and a tear trickled down her cheek. "Sam's more like a son to us than an employee. I don't know if I can stand to lose a second child."

Sarah saw the pain the remembered loss of Ruth and Orville's only son brought to her aunt's eyes. "Sam's grandfather knew the spirit of a snow wolf, remember," she reminded her aunt, then added, "besides, he's too mean to die before he's ready to."

"You take the walkie-talkie and call me every half hour," Ruth stipulated. "If I don't hear from you, I'll organize a search party if I have to lead it myself."

"Don't worry, I'll be fine," Sarah assured her once again.

"This is great . . . just great!" Sarah muttered under her breath using anger in an attempt to ignore the growing fear she didn't want to admit to. "I thought you weren't supposed to start until after dark or maybe even tomorrow," she grumbled at the snowflakes falling fast around her. Momentarily, she considered turning back but she was closer to the line shack than the ranch.

"The nearest shelter is the smartest choice," she said, repeating the advice her grandfather had issued a hundred times. Besides, she couldn't get the picture of Sam lying in the shack injured and freezing to death out of her mind.

A sudden wave of panic swept through her as the shack disappeared from her image and she saw him lying in the snow. "He made it to the shack," she growled at herself and pushed this last image from her mind.

Trying not to think of Sam, she turned her attention to her horse. "Sorry I brought you out on such a lousy day," she said, apologizing to the mare and giving it a brisk rub on the neck.

The roan snorted and gave her head a toss.

A friskiness in the horse's step seemed to imply the animal was actually enjoying this, Sarah thought. Again she patted the mare's neck and noted the heavy mat of winter hair protecting the beast. "Seems like your coat is warmer than mine," she said, taking the reins in one hand so she could adjust her scarf to cover the lower portion of her face.

The horse gave another snort as they continued on.

Sarah had hoped the snowfall would slacken after a few minutes but it continued to fall heavy and fast. About an inch every fifteen minutes, she judged. She was having trouble seeing ahead to find the landmarks she needed to keep her going in the right direction.

The snow coated her and she brushed it off but not before its wetness began to seep into her clothing. "If we don't get to that line shack soon, we're going to have to look for alternative shelter," she informed the horse, finding some comfort in communicating with another living animal.

Again the roan snorted as if in response.

Maybe she had forgotten how to get to the line shack, Sarah admitted as the coldness cut into her and doubts assailed her. This really was a stupid trek, she admonished herself. The snowstorm had slowed her progress greatly. What was worse, it was masking the remaining daylight, darkening the landscape as if dusk had already fallen and night was close behind. She was going to have to seek that alternate shelter and build a fire before her fingers and toes froze. Rising in the saddle, she scanned the horizon.

Her gaze narrowed. She could have sworn she saw a hint of light and a whiff of smoke. Hoping it wasn't just wishful thinking, she looked harder. Ahead to her right she was sure she could make out the outline of a tiny single-room cabin. It was the line shack! Even more reassuring, she could see the dark shapes of several steers and a horse huddled in and around the lean-to of the adjacent corral. "Looks like I've also found Sam Raven," she muttered, the panic she'd been fighting subsiding.

As she drew nearer to the cabin, her heart began to race and a feeling of anticipation caused her body to tense. She frowned. She was acting as if she was actually looking forward to seeing him. Her frown deepened. Sam Raven was the last person she'd come back here to see. She was simply relieved to discover that he was sheltered, she reasoned to explain this unexpected reaction.

"Sarah!" Ruth's voice came over the intercom. "Have you found the line shack yet?"

"Yes," she replied and heard an audible sigh of relief from the other end. "I can see cattle and a horse in the corral and there's smoke coming from the chimney. It's my guess Sam's inside."

"Thank goodness." Ruth's voice became stern. "Now you get yourself inside as soon as possible."

"I plan to," Sarah replied and shoved the walkie-talkie back into its holster slung on her hip. Still a hesitation swept through her as she came abreast of the cabin. I can't believe I'm still allowing the man to intimidate me so much, I'd linger in this cold rather than face him, she scolded herself silently.

Abruptly the door opened and she drew the mare to a halt as Sam's form filled the doorway. He was just as she remembered . . . broad shoulders, firm abdomen, no potbelly hanging over his belt buckle.

"Who the hell are you and what are you doing on Perry land?" he growled in a lazy drawl, standing with a rifle laying idly over his arm.

She knew that relaxed pose was purely for show. It was a mistake for anyone to underestimate Sam. "You could be a gentleman for once and ask me in. It's freezing out here," she returned tartly.

For a brief moment his composure slipped and she saw surprise on his face. "Sarah?" In the next instant his surprise was replaced by anger. "I can't believe Orville let you go riding on a day like this."

She met his scowl with one of her own. "I'm not out for an afternoon jaunt. I came looking for you. Orville's got the flu and both he and Ruth are worried to death about you. The sheriff couldn't come looking until tomorrow, so I decided to check on you myself."

"You could have frozen to death," he retorted. "Get off that horse and get in here."

She wanted to comply but her legs felt like lead weights and she had grave doubts she could swing her right one over the back of the horse. But, deciding that she'd rather fall off than ask for his help, she shook her feet loose from the stirrups. She'd hoped to slip gracefully off the horse's back. Instead, as she shifted her weight and ordered her right leg to swing over the saddle, her whole body began to slid. Knowing it was useless to try to stop herself, she released her remaining hold on the saddle horn and landed on her back in the snow. The horse balked and reared, startled by her fall.

Immediately Sam was there, calming the animal and glaring down at her. "Don't try to move," he ordered. "I'll check you for injuries as soon as I've got this horse under control."

She wiggled her toes and fingers. All twenty were nearly frozen but they worked. "I'm fine," she tossed back, ignoring his order and pushing herself to her feet.

"Sarah? Did you find Sam?" Ruth's voice came over the walkie-talkie.

"Yes," she replied, clumsily getting the communicator out with her stiff fingers. "I found him and he hasn't changed a bit."

Ruth breathed an audible sigh. "Stay inside and stay warm."

"Will do," Sarah managed to say, the thought of spending hours closeted with Sam causing her stomach to tighten. The man was arrogant and intimidating and he didn't like her. So what's new? she chided herself as she again pocketed the walkie-talkie.

Continuing to stand stiffly, waiting for more feeling to return to her legs before she tried to actually walk, she returned her attention to Sam. "I'll unsaddle my horse and put him in the corral in a minute."

"I'll take care of your horse." Sam strode to the door, reached inside and pulled out his coat. As he slipped it on, he again frowned at her. "Go inside."

"I'll go inside when I'm ready to go inside," she returned.

A sudden look of understanding crossed his face and he scowled. "Why don't you just admit you can't walk."

Before she could think of a protest that wasn't a lie, Sarah felt herself being scooped up and tossed over his shoulder like a sack of flour.

"Keep your head down," he ordered as he strode through the doorway. Once inside, he set her on her feet in front of the fireplace then eased her into the rocking chair by the hearth. "I'll be back as soon as I've taken care of the mare," he said, then left.

Sarah sat staring into the fire. Her body felt like an icicle. She felt like an idiot. Sam hadn't needed any help. "His grandfather knew the spirit of a snow wolf," she muttered to the flames. "He's probably thriving on this weather."

As feeling returned to her body, she began to shiver. Sam had always had a knack for making her feel foolish, she thought acidly, trying to ignore her discomfort.

"You're soaked."

She looked to the door, to see that the source of her anger had returned. "So tell me something I don't know," she returned.

His expression grim, he kicked the door closed with his booted heel. In two long strides, he crossed to the rough-hewn wooden table near the center of the room, dropped her saddlebags and bedroll on it, then strode across the room to the door. He took off his coat and hat and hung them on the pegs that were nailed to the wall near the entrance.

Then he turned back to her. "Give me your coat."

Using the arms of the chair, Sarah forced herself to stand. "I can hang up my own clothing, thank you." Her whole body felt somewhat numb and she had to concentrate hard to make her hands work, but she managed to take off her gloves.

"Damn it, Sarah, a fall from a horse combined with being nearly frozen to death will shake up anyone."

She looked at him to see him watching her with impatient anger. Then before she could respond, he'd strode to her and was unfastening the holster holding the walkie-talkie. Tossing that aside, he turned his attention to her coat.

"You always hated asking for help," he grumbled as he finished unbuttoning the heavy parka.

"Only from you." The admission slipped out unexpectedly. She hid her embarrassment behind a cool mask.

A stoic expression descended over his features. "We always did seem to get on each other nerves."

The indifference with which he accepted the fact that they would never be friends, caused an old familiar pang deep inside. Why she had ever cared about being his friend was a mystery to her, she chided herself and ignored the uncomfortable twinge.

He was removing her coat now and she shifted her shoulders to aid him. His fingers brushed against her shirt. A startling current of heat seemed to radiate from his touch and travel down her arms. *My body is just so cold any warmth seems exaggerated*, she reasoned as he finished slipping her coat from her.

Lumps of snow fell at her feet. Obviously when she'd fallen some of the cold wet stuff had packed itself under her coat. Now she realized that everything, even her undergarments, had gotten wet to some degree. She shifted closer to the fire.

"You're soaked to the bone. You're going to have to strip."

Sarah jerked around to find Sam regarding her with continued impatience as if he found her presence here a burden he was not happy about being forced to bear.

"I'll dry," she replied frostily, and returned her attention to the fire.

"You'll catch pneumonia and I'll have to leave the cattle here to die from hunger just so I can get you back to the ranch," he growled. He'd moved to the table and was freeing her bedroll from its waterproof covering. After shaking out the sleeping bag, he unzipped it, then tossed it onto the rocking chair. His gaze leveled on her. "We can do this one of two ways. You can strip on your own or I'll do it for you."

The sudden image of him removing her clothes caused a curl of excitement. *This cold has affected my* mind, she ridiculed herself. "You and what army?" she snapped back.

The impatience on his face grew stronger. "I promise I'll be the perfect gentleman. Just get out of those wet things."

His assurance had the sting of an insult. Her back stiffened more, but before she could again refuse to get out of her wet clothing, she stopped herself. He was right. She was feeling more and more chilled by the moment. "Turn your back," she ordered.

She caught the flash of relief in his eyes as he obeyed. Clearly he was not making an idle threat when he said he'd strip her if she didn't do it herself. However, it was equally clear that he had not relished the idea. Arrogant bore, she thought haughtily and began removing her clothing.

Her fingers were working better now and she was able to strip without any real difficulty. As soon as she'd discarded the last of her clothing, she wrapped herself in the sleeping bag. "All right, I'm decent," she announced primly.

Sam turned as she bent to pick up one of the short benches beside the table.

"What are you doing now?" he demanded.

"I'm going to put this bench over by the fire and lay my clothes on it so they'll dry," she replied, allowing her own impatience at having her actions questioned to show.

"You sit. I'll move the bench and spread out your clothes," he commanded.

She glanced up, intending to tell him she didn't need or want his help, but the words died in her throat. For one brief moment, before his impassive mask had again descended over his features, she was sure she'd glimpsed something that looked very much like desire in the dark depths of his eyes. But it was her body's answering response that truly shook her. Her heart seemed to pause, then began beating wildly and a glow of pleasure warmed her. "If you insist," she heard herself saying and, releasing the bench, returned to the rocking chair.

Forcing herself not to stare, she studied him covertly as he set the bench nearer the fire then spread her clothing out on it. She saw his jaw twitch in an outward show of discomfort when he arranged her undergarments. Any feelings she was stirring in him were ones he didn't want, she realized, and the warm glow vanished.

Leaning back in the rocking chair, she closed her eyes. The old memory that had threatened to surface today once before, now came sharply into focus. She was seventeen and Sam was nineteen. She'd gone out for an afternoon ride. Her grandfather had insisted Sam go along to watch over her. She'd assured her grandfather that she'd be fine but he'd been adamant.

As usual, Sam had been stoic, accepting the assignment with an air of indifference. But she knew he didn't want to baby-sit her.

His uncle, Wild Coyote, had worked part-time for her grandfather for years. About the time Sam had turned twelve, Wild Coyote had started bringing Sam to the ranch with him. The original intent, Sarah had gathered, was for Sam to be a companion to Ruth and

Orville's son. They were both the same age and Orville Junior didn't have any nearby playmates.

But Sam had different plans. He'd come to work. At first, her grandfather had found small tasks for him to perform. He was a quick learner and a hard worker. Her grandfather had been impressed and when Sam turned sixteen, her grandfather had hired him on as a wrangler for the summers.

From the first day Sam and Sarah had met, he'd made a point of staying as far away from her as possible. Thus, she had been absolutely certain he would rather have been staring a rattlesnake in the eye than riding with her. However, trying to make the best of an uncomfortable situation, she'd attempted to make light conversation but his answers had been monosyllabic and she'd given up.

After half an hour of riding in silence with him following about ten feet behind, she'd considered cutting her ride short. But this was her first day back at the ranch after having spent the summer with her brother Lester helping to take care of her young niece Eloise. She'd loved being with Eloise but she'd missed this untamed land and the feeling of oneness with nature she experienced when she rode far enough out onto it to feel as if she'd left all civilization behind.

The thought that Sam Raven was part of that civilization she was trying to escape had suddenly flashed through her mind. She doubted her horse could outrun his but, reasoning that a fast gallop might get rid of the tension she was still feeling as well as let her forget his company for at least a brief time, she had given her mount a nudge.

Exhilaration had filled her as the mare ran full out. Glancing over her shoulder, she'd seen Sam keeping pace just enough to remain ten feet behind. A grim look of disapproval was on his face. But then, he rarely seemed to approve of anything she did, she'd reminded herself, and ignored him.

She had finally begun to enjoy her ride and the urge to laugh out loud was almost irrepressible when a low rumbling filled the air. She had reined her horse in and looked toward the west. A huge thunderhead was headed their way. Lightning flashed straight down to the ground. Behind her, she'd heard Sam utter a curse.

"Guess we'd better get back to the ranch," she'd said, turning her horse toward home.

Sam blocked her way with his mount. "We'll never make it. The line shack's closer." He kicked his horse back to a gallop and she'd followed.

They'd made it to the shack just far enough ahead of the storm to get the horses into the lean-to and themselves into the small, single-room cabin before the rain began. It had come in a torrent—drops so huge she saw them splash when they hit. The ground shook as a bright jagged streak of lightning shot down from the sky to touch it.

The horses whined with fear and Sam strode to the door.

Out of the corner of her eye, Sarah saw him. She'd been standing at one of the two small windows, watching the fury outside. "You can't go out in that," she'd said, catching his sleeve as he reached for the door.

"I have to check on the horses," he'd returned, jerking free.

"They're fine. I can see them." She motioned for him to look out the window.

He scowled but obeyed her unspoken invitation. It was then that it had occurred to her that he'd rather be in that lean-to with the horses than in the cabin with her. Anger welled up inside of her. "Of course, if you'd rather be out there in this rain, be my guest," she said dryly.

For a moment she thought he might actually choose to do just that, then shrugging, he'd continued to stand looking out the window. His expression was unreadable, still she couldn't shake the feeling that he wished he was anywhere but there with her. The heavy silence between them grated on her nerves.

"Some people find my company pleasant," she blurted cuttingly. "Ward Anders wrote me nearly every day while I was gone."

Impatience had showed on his face. "Then you should have invited him to go riding with you."

"I wanted to be alone." The dryness returned to her voice. "Of course, being with you is pretty close to that."

Accepting this last jab with a shrug of indifference, he turned his attention back to the view beyond the window. Again a silence fell between them.

The storm outside increased in strength, blocking out the sun and causing the day to darken. Bolts of lightning, coming close together, pierced the sky. Ground-jarring thunder followed almost immediately. The air seemed charged with electricity. Sarah had moved to the window on the other side of the door, putting distance between her and Sam.

"Your grandfather was right. You do need someone to look after you," he suddenly growled.

Startled that he'd spoken, Sarah turned to him. He was still looking out the window. Her back stiffened with defiance. "I—"

"You could have broken your neck, letting your horse run the way you did," he said, interrupting her protest. He turned toward her then. "When we start back, I want you to keep a moderate pace. This rain will cause a lot of washing and the footing for the horses could be unsteady."

His patronizing manner caused her already taut nerves to snap. "I'd be flattered if I thought your concern was for me. But it's my guess it's my mare you're really worried about."

He reached her in three long strides. "I don't want to see you get hurt." His hands closed around her upper arms. "You've got to be the most bullheaded female ever put on the face of this earth." His hold tightened. "I want your word, you'll ride easy."

His attempt to boss her raised her ire even more. If he'd honestly cared about her, she wouldn't have minded. But knowing that he could barely stand her company only flamed the fires of her resentment. That he was right about the rain didn't seem to matter.

She glared up at him intending to tell him that she wasn't stupid and knew how to be careful and didn't need his advice. But the words caught in her throat. His expression was cold and grim but when her eyes met his she suddenly found herself staring into a fire so intense it caused her legs to weaken. "Sam?" she breathed his name questioningly.

The heat in his eyes intensified. He drew her toward him and his mouth found hers. She'd been kissed before but it had never felt like this. Every fiber of her being was aware of his touch. Her blood raced and she wished he wasn't holding her by the arms so she could move closer to him. Being nearer to him seemed almost like a need.

Then abruptly, he'd jerked away from her. An expression of self-reproach was etched deeply into his features. "Sorry. That should never have happened," he said gruffly, then stalked back to the other window and stood staring outside.

For a long moment, she was too stunned to speak. When she did find her voice she was only able to manage a quiet, "Sam?"

"My grandfather is a shaman. My father is a shaman. My grandmother has predicted that I will be called also. When that happens, I will return to the reservation and remain among my people. Out of respect to my ancestors and in accordance with my grandmother's wishes, I will take an Indian wife."

There had been a finality in his voice as if this prophecy of his future was carved in stone. Still, the urge to protest it was strong. But Sarah was too confused to speak. She'd never felt such an intense attraction to a man before and for that man to be Sam Raven shocked her.

They'd barely spoken the remainder of that afternoon. When the storm broke, Sam motioned her out of the cabin. They rode back to the ranch in silence.

She'd had a date with Ward that night. But her mind had been preoccupied with the memory of Sam's kiss. She'd finally pleaded a headache and had Ward take her home early.

Sam had been sitting on the porch of the bunkhouse whittling when she'd gotten back to the ranch. She started over to talk to him, but he'd gotten up and gone inside, letting her know he preferred they kept their distance.

After a week of being avoided by him, she'd convinced herself her strong reaction to his kiss had been merely a result of the added electrical energy of the storm. Then they'd nearly collided in the barn. Immediately her blood had begun to race. But there had been a guarded expression on his face as if he feared she might embarrass them both by throwing herself at him. Pride had come to her rescue. "You're much too bullheaded for any woman to want to spend a lifetime with." She'd spit out the words and strode away.

After that she'd turned her full attention again to Ward.

# Chapter Two

Sarah's stomach growled, bringing her mind back to the present. Teenage lust can be a strong memory; she mocked herself for even recalling the kiss.

"I'm boiling a rabbit," Sam said, squatting by the fire and lifting the lid off an iron pot sitting partway in the coals. "It should be ready soon."

"Smells good," she conceded, her stomach growling again. Considering his less than enthusiastic welcome, she disliked accepting anything from him. Then she remembered she had something to contribute to the meal and her pride was appeased. She nodded toward the saddlebags. "Ruth sent along some provisions."

"Figured that was the case." Rising in one lithe movement, he walked to the table.

Sarah wanted to ignore him. But like a magnet drawn to due north, her gaze followed him. There was a strength in the way he carried himself that let her know he had added no flab to his frame.

His thick black hair hung well below his shoulder blades. But he wore no headband. Instead his hair was pulled back and gathered with a leather thong into a ponytail at his nape. She noted that, like herself, he had a few gray strands to mark his years.

Her attention focused on his face. His features had matured into a ruggedly handsome countenance. Grim, but handsome, she amended, wondering if he ever smiled. She guessed she could count on one hand the times she'd seen him smile in their youth. He was then and was still now, the personification of the stoic, aloof Indian brave, she thought.

"Well?"

She jumped slightly at the abruptness with which he'd turned to her and spoken. "Well, what?" she replied in confusion.

"You've been taking an inventory. Have you reached any conclusions?" he demanded gruffly.

Clearly he'd felt her studying him and hadn't liked it. Embarrassed to have been caught, she considered lying and pretending she didn't know what he was talking about. But cowardliness, she admonished herself, was for youngsters and she was no longer a youngster. "You've aged well," she replied with schooled nonchalance. Then, forcing herself to move with slow dignity as if she'd finished her inspection and was no longer interested, she turned her attention back to the fire.

A trickle of water on the back of her neck let her know that her own long black tresses were more than a little wet and most likely dampening her bedroll. Moving carefully to ensure her modesty, she freed her arms and shoulders then unwound the single braid hanging down the middle of her back. Once her hair was loose, she combed it out with her fingers, then leaning toward the fire combed it forward over her head so that it was arrayed toward the warmth.

"You've aged well, too," Sam said, breaking the silence between them.

Through the cascade of her tresses she saw him setting a coffeepot in the coals. He wasn't looking at her but there was an honesty in his voice that rang true. A flush of pleasure brought a tint of pink to her cheeks. Then her eyes focused nearer and she saw a couple of the gray strands that now lightly salted her hair. "But sometimes I do feel old."

He glanced over his shoulder at her. "You look like a woman in her prime to me."

Sarah peeked at him through her hair. There was nothing flirtatious in his voice or manner. His expression was cool and controlled as if he was merely stating a fact. And because she knew he wasn't the kind to indulge in idle flattery, the glow of pleasure returned. "Thanks."

He shrugged. "No need to thank a person for telling the truth," he said as he rose and went back to the table to sort through the rest of the supplies Ruth had sent.

As silence descended between them once again, Sarah combed her fingers through her hair. It was getting dry. A blast of cold wind rattled the windows and caused the door to creak loudly as if the elements were trying to break in on them. She frowned. She should feel at least a little bit of trepidation but instead she felt cozy and safe. That she could feel comfortable, even cozy, in Sam Raven's presence amazed her. I'm just glad to be inside instead of out in that storm, she reasoned.

"The military seems to have been a good life for you," Sam said, breaking into her thoughts.

Startled that he'd spoken yet again, she studied him covertly as he put more wood on the fire. "It was. They sent me to nursing school so I learned a profession. And I had several overseas assignments. Join the navy and see the world . . . that's what they say."

As she spoke, Sam pulled a straight-back chair nearer to the fire, then picked up a piece of wood that was beginning to resemble the shape of a bird and began to carve it. After a moment or two, he said in an easy drawl, "Heard you'd been seeing the world since you got out, too."

He had changed some, she noted. He was actually encouraging a conversation. "A little," she replied. "I never did like being idle. Within a couple of weeks after I retired, I went and signed up with a private nursing agency. They had connections with the movie and television studios and pretty soon I was getting offers of assignments all over the world looking after injured directors and actors." You're rattling on, she admonished herself and clamped her mouth shut.

Sam flicked a large shaving into the fire. "So you're just here for a visit between assignments?"

Sarah continued to frown at the flames. Ward's face filled her inner vision. An uneasiness stirred within her. Maybe coming back here hadn't been such a great idea. Thomas Wolfe warned about the changes time can cause. I've got to face the past before I can get on with a future, she told herself. Aloud she said, "Yes, it's been a long time since I've seen Ruth and Orville and they're getting on in age."

Sam paused in his whittling to study her dryly. "Couldn't be that Ward Ander's being widowed a couple of years ago has anything to do with your coming back, could it?"

Sarah caught the taunting edge in his voice. This was the Sam she knew well...the one who seemed to disapprove of nearly everything she did. Well, she wouldn't lie to him. Somehow, he'd learn the truth. He always did. She faced him squarely. "Could be. I won't know until I see him."

A self-congratulating smirk for guessing right played across his face, then he turned his attention back to his whittling.

His "I knew it" attitude grated on her nerves. Well, he wasn't always right about everything, she reminded herself. "I'm sort of surprised you're still here," she said coolly.

He looked up questioningly. "Only a fool would venture out in this storm."

"I meant here at this ranch," she elaborated. "I thought you were merely waiting for your call as a shaman, then you were going to vanish back to the reservation, never to be seen by any of us here again."

He grinned sheepishly at the melodramatic picture he'd once painted of his intentions. "It seems my grandmother was wrong about my future."

Her first reaction to his outward show of embarrassment was surprise. She'd been certain that nothing she could say or do would affect him in any way. Suddenly feeling as if she'd behaved childishly, mocking his hoped for future, she said honestly, "I'm sorry."

"I'm not." Setting aside his carving, he met her gaze levelly. "My life suits me just fine. I like ranching and I'm better with animals than with people." His gaze abruptly shifted to the pot by the fire. "The rabbit and coffee should be ready now."

He was definitely better with animals than with people, she agreed mentally as he served up the food and handed her a plate and mug.

They ate in silence.

When she finished, she carried her plate to the table. Then before reseating herself, she poured herself another cup of coffee. "Want some?" she asked politely, over her shoulder.

"No," he replied tersely, never taking his eyes off his carving.

She saw his jaw twitch in an outward sign of agitation and knew her company was again wearing on his nerves. The thought that he'd rather be trapped here a month alone than spend one night cloistered with her played through her mind. Her ire again rose. "Next time remember to take a walkie-talkie along and you won't get stuck with company you don't want," she advised caustically as she reseated herself.

"I'll keep that in mind," he replied, continuing to concentrate on his whittling.

Sarah awoke shivering. Her clothes hadn't dried by the time she and Sam had turned in for the night. He'd insisted she take the single narrow cot and had pulled it near the fire. But the fire had died and even snuggled in the cocoon of her bedroll, she was cold.

Sam was lying on the floor nearby sound asleep. Keeping her bedroll around her and being careful not to step on him, she eased herself off the cot and put more wood on the fire. To her relief the coals were still red-hot and tossing a pile of kindling on them brought the flames back up and caught the larger logs.

Climbing back onto the cot a few minutes later, she congratulated herself for not waking Sam. By the time they'd retired for the night, the tension in the cabin had grown until her nerves were near the snapping point. He'd made her feel like a weed in his flower garden and she was in no mood for more of the same.

"You must be carrying a mighty hot torch for Anders to have remained single all these years." His voice suddenly cut through the stillness between them.

Silently she cursed under her breath. She could have sworn he'd been asleep. "I suppose," she heard herself admitting, too tired to be anything but honest.

"It'll never work. You're too strong-willed a woman for him."

Sarah glared down at the man on the floor as he yawned, closed his eyes and turned his back to her once again. She knew he'd never liked Ward and if he'd said that she and Ward deserved each other or would make a great pair, she could have ignored his observation. Instead his words touched a raw nerve within her. "I am not as difficult to get along with as you seem to think. Has it ever occurred to you that maybe you're the one who it's so impossible to be civil to?"

He turned back to her. "I didn't say you were difficult to get along with. What I was trying to point out was that you're an independent woman. It's been my observation that Anders likes people around him he can rule. You've never struck me as the kind of person who would be comfortable under someone's thumb. Heard you made it all the way to the rank of commander before you retired."

Sarah frowned at him. "All successful marriages require some compromise. There's a big difference between compromising and being ruled," she argued back.

"There sure is and if I were you I'd make real sure which one I was agreeing to before I made any commitments," he returned. "'Night," he added and rolled over, marking an end to this discussion.

Sarah glared at his back. She didn't need Sam Raven telling her how to run her life. Shifting onto her back, she stared up at the ceiling. She'd come back home hoping to find the cure for the void within her that seemed to be growing steadily with each passing day and she refused to allow an arrogant cowhand to stir up doubts for her success before she'd even begun. "He who hesitates is lost," she murmured.

"Only a fool enters unexplored territory without being careful to scout the lay of the land first," he rebutted quietly.

"I know how to reconnoiter," Sarah snapped and braced herself for his next shot. Instead a silence descended over the cabin. He'd let her have the last word! She'd been sure he wouldn't. Still, half expecting to hear him say one last thing, she dozed off.

The delicious fragrance of food cooking filled the cabin when Sarah awoke the next time.

"Ruth sure knows how to stock saddlebags. This ham smells like one of her special home-cured ones," Sam said, glancing over his shoulder at her from his squatting position in front of the fire.

Sarah shifted uncomfortably as nature called.

Sam scooped the ham out onto a plate, then sat the skillet aside and rose. "I'll go check on the animals. Give me a call when you're ready to eat."

His consideration surprised her. The outhouse out back had been nearly covered by a drift by nightfall last night. She had no desire to plod through the snow this morning to find it. She'd expected she'd have to either ask him to step outside while she used the primitive facilities, namely a bucket with a wooden lid, available in the cabin, or try to use it as discreetly as possible with his back turned to her. "Thanks," she said gratefully.

He nodded, pulled on his coat and left.

Moving as quickly as possible, she relieved her discomfort and dressed. Her clothes had dried fairly well. Just the legs of her jeans remained slightly damp. As soon as she was decent, she opened the door and looked outside.

The sun was breaking over the horizon, its light reflecting off the new-fallen snow. At least six more inches had fallen during the night, adding to what was already on the ground. Sam was in the corral with the animals, checking to see how they'd fared through the night. "You can come in and eat now," she called out.

He waved back to let her know he'd heard, then giving her mare a rub on the neck, he started back to the cabin.

Closing the door and walking over to the fire, it occurred to Sarah that she should be at least a little apprehensive. They had a difficult ride back to the ranch. Instead she felt invigorated. In fact, she admitted, she hadn't felt this alive in a long time.

"Nor looked so unkempt," she added, catching a glimpse of herself in the small shaving mirror hanging on the wall. Her hair was a tangled mass. Remembering that she hadn't brought along a brush, she combed some order into the tresses with her fingers then loosely braided them into a single pigtail at the back of her neck.

Sam had entered and discarded his coat and hat while she was working on her hair. Now he was kneeling by the fire, pouring a couple of cups of coffee. The air in the cabin seemed suddenly charged and she frowned at herself for letting the man's presence affect her so strongly. It's just a knee-jerk reaction in preparation for an inevitable confrontation, she reasoned.

"You look real nice this morning...rested," he said as he rose and handed her the cup of hot brew.

She came close to spilling her coffee as a warm glow of pleasure spread through her. "That sounded almost like a compliment."

"Just saying what I see," he replied.

What she saw was uneasiness in his eyes and the glow of pleasure faded. Knowing her hair still looked as if it needed a good brushing, that she had no makeup to soften the angular features of her face and that her clothing was a mass of wrinkles, she chided herself for falling prey to a bit of fluff flattery. Obviously Sam was merely trying to be polite under difficult circumstances and wasn't really sure how to go about it. "Why don't you just think of me as one of the wranglers," she suggested.

He grinned crookedly. "That's a little hard. You've got too many curves in the right places."

The masculine appreciation she read on his face heated her blood. She found herself wondering how his arms would feel around her and how his lips would feel on hers.

His dark gaze grew warmer as if he could read her thoughts. Her hand trembled and some coffee spilt, burning her fingers. The pain caused her to break her gaze from his. Sanity abruptly returned. Me and Rumbling Thunder? she mocked herself, taking a step back from him as he started toward her. She'd come to Wyoming to find a loving companion with whom to share her life, not a sparring partner.

"I just wanted to see how badly you were burned," he said curtly.

"It's not bad at all," she replied stiffly, still shaken by how much she'd wanted him to kiss her. Her gaze flickered over his strong form and a fresh rush of heat swept through her. She still wanted him to kiss her. Again she reminded herself, she'd come here searching for a relationship to fill a void in her life, not one that would give her an ulcer.

He scowled impatiently. Turning, he went to the door and stepped outside. In a moment he returned with a handful of snow. "Put this on the burn," he ordered.

His manner was businesslike and impersonal. She noticed the heat had completely gone from his eyes. In its place was the cool aloofness she remembered so well. He'd felt nothing but a momentary lust, she realized and congratulated herself for not allowing herself to give in to a moment of insanity that she would have regretted afterward. "Really, my hand is fine," she insisted.

"Stubborn as a mule," he muttered under his breath, taking her coffee mug from her and pressing the snow to her hand.

The cold soothed the remaining burning sensation where the coffee had spilt. But she barely noticed the relief. It was his hard, callused palms that held her attention. There was an enticing strength in their rough, textured touch. Drawing a shaky breath, she gently but firmly freed her hand. "We should eat before the fire dies and the ham gets cold."

"You're right," he agreed, freeing her immediately and going to the hearth where the metal plate holding the ham sat near the coals being kept warm.

Sarah had the distinct feeling he'd been relieved to have an excuse to break the contact. Even if our lives depended on it, I doubt he and I could remain civil to each other for more than an hour at a time, she thought dryly and ordered herself to quickly squelch any further insane romantic notions that might enter her mind.

Concentrating only on food, she busied herself helping to gather the rest of their breakfast together. Ruth had also sent along some biscuits and a can of beans, which they ate with the ham.

"The cattle should be fine here for a couple of days," Sam said as they finished. "I'll get you back to the ranch, then come back for them."

Still somewhat unnerved by the mixture of emotions he aroused in her, Sarah had been avoiding looking at him. Now she met his gaze with a reproving frown. "You can't be serious. Another storm front could move into this area. And, even if it didn't, only a fool would make this trip more times than was absolutely necessary."

His jaw set with purpose. "Taking those cattle will make the trip at least a couple of hours longer. And there's no telling what trouble they might get into. I don't want to have to worry about them and you, too."

Again he made her feel like an annoyance. Her shoulders straightened. "You don't have to worry about me. And I can wrangle as good as any man."

"You've never herded cattle through snow. They can do real stupid things sometimes," he growled.

Unexpectedly the image of him hurt and lying freezing in a deep drift filled her mind. This was followed by a rush of fear so intense that bile rose in her throat. She'd hate to see anyone die that way, she told herself, attempting to justify the strength of her reaction. "No more stupid than you coming out here alone without even taking the walkie-talkie," she shot back.

"I know what I'm doing. It's my job. Times are tough. This ranch can't afford to lose this many head of cattle. But I need to get you home first."

Seeing that his jaw was still firm, Sarah chose another ploy. Sam, she knew, did not make friends easily. But when he did, he would stand by that friend through the fires of hell. And, she was pretty sure, he considered Orville and Ruth friends of that kind. "If you take me back to the ranch without the cattle, Orville is certain to insist on coming back out here with you. He's got the flu and the trip would, most likely, kill him."

The mention of her uncle brought an expression of deep concern to Sam's face. His jaw tightened and Sarah had the distinct impression he was holding a mental debate with himself. His expression grew grimmer. For a moment he looked as if he was going to continue arguing, then he nodded. "You're right. Let's get moving."

Breathing a silent sigh of relief, Sarah quickly began gathering their dishes and utensils. The sooner they were back at the ranch, the sooner she could get on with her real purpose for returning to Anders Butte.

\* \* \*

"You take the right flank. I'll take the left," Sam called out to her. Sarah was mounted, waiting on the outside of the corral while Sam drove the cattle out. She waved back in acknowledgment. A sense of excitement stirred within her as the animals began to move through the gate. She had forgotten just how much she'd enjoyed ranch work. There was something truly invigorating about herding cattle astride horseback.

But it was definitely hard work, she groaned mentally a couple of hours later. And cold, she added. Luckily the cows were basically cooperating and moving steadily. "But there's always one who's a problem," she muttered, seeing a cow a few feet ahead of her turn away from the others and strike out on its own.

Urging her horse to move faster, she caught up with the beast and turned it back to rejoin the others. Feeling proud of her show of competence, she'd found herself glancing toward Sam to see if he'd noticed but he was cursing at a cow on his flank who had decided to stop and try to paw through the snow for food.

A jab of disappointment pierced her. The realization that she'd been looking for his approval shook her. It's not *his* approval, she assured herself. She was simply proud of herself and wanted someone to have witnessed her feat. Of course, he could have probably done what she did blindfolded, she mocked her burst of pride and ordered herself to once again concentrate on her job.

By the time the ranch came into view, she had to admit her exhilaration had worn thin and a warm room and hot cup of coffee sounded like heaven.

"I'll drive these animals back into the rest of the herd," Sam called out to her. "You go on in."

She was very tempted but she hated leaving a job half done. Besides, she knew he had to be as cold and tired as she was. "I've come this far, I'll go the rest of the way," she replied, and stayed on her flank as they steered the cattle toward the fenced field just beyond the barn that was used for wintering the beasts.

Sam looked as if he was going to argue, then giving a shrug to indicate he'd decided he'd be wasting his breath, he gave his horse a nudge and rode a little ahead to open the gate.

When the last cow passed through and Sam reached down to fasten the gate, Sarah drew a satisfied breath and turned her horse toward the barn. But as she reached the barn and reined her horse in, she realized her legs had grown stiff. Mentally she pictured herself making another falling dismount. She glanced toward the house, hoping Ruth wouldn't be there to witness her clumsy descent. To her chagrin, her aunt stepped out on the back porch and waved. She waved back and to her relief, Ruth went back inside.

"Well, I can't sit here all day," she muttered under her breath. But before she could make her leg attempt to swing over the saddle, the sound of a horse approaching caused her to glance over her shoulder. She'd waited too long! Sam was coming. She'd just have to wait until he dismounted and took his horse into the barn, she decided, and leaned forward to stroke and talk to her mare as if having a serious conversation with the animal.

"You planning to sit there all afternoon?" Sam asked as he swung out of the saddle.

"I was just thanking her for being so good," Sarah replied haughtily. She expected him to continue on into the barn, but instead he continued to regard her thoughtfully.

"Legs a little stiff?"

She considered lying but that was something a foolish young girl would do, she mocked herself. And she was no longer young and she hoped she was not a fool. "A little," she admitted grudgingly.

Before she realized what was happening, Sam had approached her and placed his hands around her waist. "Kick your feet free from the stirrups," he ordered.

Deciding that getting down from the horse and inside the house where it was warm was more important than her pride, she did as he commanded.

"Now put your hands on my shoulders," he directed.

In spite of her determination to notice him as little as possible, she found herself thinking that he certainly had sturdy shoulders. Then she felt herself being eased off the horse and lowered to the ground. Her legs felt rubbery when her weight was placed on them and her hands tightened their hold.

His grip on her waist had slackened when she touched the ground; now it became firm once again. "Can you stand?"

She looked up to see worry etched into his features. Then it turned to self-directed anger. "I knew I shouldn't have let you insist on driving those cattle back. You probably have frostbite."

His self-recrimination mingled with a protectiveness that caused a warm glow deep within. "I don't have frostbite. It's just been a long time since I sat in a saddle that long." She shifted from one foot to the other. "I can walk just fine now."

"You did a good job today," he said gruffly.

A flush of pleasure reddened her cheeks. "I enjoyed it."

His gaze bore into her. "You really did?"

She read the surprise in his eyes. "I had forgotten how much I loved ranching," she heard herself adding.

"It gets into a person's blood," he replied.

A heat was beginning to warm the dark depths of his eyes and she found herself being drawn into the flames. Suddenly she was acutely aware that his hands were still around her waist and her own hands were still holding onto his shoulders. Her gaze was now locked into his and she knew that he was going to kiss her. And in the next minute they'd be fighting, she warned herself. That wasn't the kind of relationship she'd come here to find! "I think we should get our horses into the barn and unsaddled," she said, jerking her gaze from his.

For a brief second he continued to hold her captive, then abruptly released her. "You're right." He reached for her reins. "I'll take care of the horses, you go inside."

His tone was coolly polite as if speaking to a mere acquaintance. There was no hint that there had been a moment of attraction between them. She looked up at him to find his expression impassive. Maybe I just imagined he was thinking of kissing me, she decided. But the feeling had been strong. Whatever happened, it was best forgotten. "I am cold," she admitted, suddenly needing to put distance between herself and this man.

Without looking back she headed to the house and a hot cup of coffee.

# Chapter Three

"Well, you're sure a sight for sore eyes," Ruth greeted Sarah happily at the back door. "Hearing your voice over the walkie-talkie helped ease my worry, but seeing you home safe is a relief."

"It feels good to be here," Sarah replied, returning her aunt's hug. The lingering smells of cooking filled the air. In spite of the fact that Sam had insisted she chew on beef jerky to keep her strength up during the ride, her stomach felt hollow.

Taking a step back to give Sarah room to pull off her gloves and coat, Ruth's smile became a playful grin. "Ward Anders has called half a dozen times since you left. I happened to mention to Sadie Meyers at church on Sunday that we were expecting you for a visit. Guess she mentioned it to someone else and word got around to him. Anyway, he made me promise you'd call him the moment you got back. I wrote his number for you on the pad by the phone in the hall, so's you wouldn't have to look it up."

Sarah's hunger was forgotten, replaced by nervousness. "I guess I should go call him then."

"I reckon you should," Ruth agreed. "You hurry along and make that call while I finish putting together a few sandwiches for you and Sam. I know the both of you have to be nearly starving."

Sarah barely acknowledged her aunt's words as she quickly strode out into the hall. Reaching for the receiver, she noticed her hand shaking slightly. Calm down, she ordered herself as she glanced at the pad. There were two numbers: one for the bank and one for Ward's home. Guessing he'd still be at the bank, she punched in that number. Nervousness caused her to make two tries before she got it right. I'm acting like a teenager, she scolded herself as her body braced itself for the sound of his voice.

"Anders Bank, how may I help you?" a woman's voice came over the line.

"I'm returning a call from Mr. Anders," Sarah said stiffly.

"Please hold," the female voice instructed.

Sarah heard a ring, then a male voice came on the line. "Ward Anders, here," it said in a friendly, yet businesslike manner.

Sarah's nervousness multiplied. "It's Sarah...Sarah Orman."

"Sarah."

She heard the tender edge that had entered Ward's voice and a crooked smile played at the corners of her mouth. "My aunt told me you called."

"I can't believe you went out in that storm," he scolded gently. "I've been worried sick about you."

His protectiveness pleased her. "I'm flattered by your concern," she admitted honestly.

"You've been on my mind a great deal since I heard you were coming for a visit," he continued, the tenderness returning to his voice. "I was hoping you would find time to have dinner with me."

Mentally Sarah issued a shout of triumph. Maintaining an outward show of merely friendly politeness, she said, "I'd enjoy having dinner with you."

"Tomorrow night? I'll pick you up around six," he suggested coaxingly.

"Sounds like fun," she replied. She was about to ask where they would be dining when a buzz sounded in the background.

"I've got a call on another line," Ward explained apologetically. "See you at six tomorrow," he repeated, then with a quick goodbye rung off.

Sarah drew a shaky breath as she returned the receiver to its cradle. He'd sought her out and asked her for a date. That had to be a good sign. Suddenly her stomach growled and she remembered Ruth's promise of sandwiches. "I could eat a bear," she murmured, heading back into the kitchen.

"Did you reach Ward?" her aunt asked as Sarah entered.

"I'm having dinner with him tomorrow night," she replied without pausing as she continued toward the plate of sandwiches on the table.

"He sure didn't waste any time," a male voice noted dryly.

Sarah jerked around to see Sam standing at the counter to her left pouring himself a cup of coffee. "Time wasted is time lost forever," she returned with equal dryness, resuming her path to the table.

"The hunter should stalk his prey carefully or he may find himself with a trophy he does not want," Sam cautioned.

Sarah experienced a sharp jab of irritation. She and Sam Raven weren't friends. In many ways, they were barely acquaintances. Admittedly there had been a couple of momentary instances of lusty thoughts between them, but that was as far as it had gone. And he was definitely the last person whose opinion she was interested in hearing. She swallowed the bite of sandwich she had just taken and turned to him. "Chances taken can lead to endless possibilities. Chances not taken lead nowhere."

"Taking thoughtless chances can lead to the path of regret," Sam tossed back.

Sarah glared at him. "You..." she began, intending to tell him he could mind his own business.

Before she could get a second word out Ruth suddenly said, "You two remind me of Grandma Perry and Morning Dove."

Both Sam and Sarah turned to look at her.

"Your grandmother would quote an adage, sometimes a real one, sometimes one she'd just made up, and Morning Dove would come back with something that sounded like an old Indian saying." Ruth hurried on, clearly sensing a confrontation and attempting to thwart it with this reminiscence. "Each tried mightily to get the last word." She grinned at Sarah as the memory grew stronger. "You caught on to the game fast. You'd come to visit armed with batches of new adages you'd come across."

The smile faded as her attention shifted to Sam. "You, however, surprise me. Never thought I'd hear you spewing out sage advice." Her gaze narrowed on him. "'Course in this instance, I have to side with Sarah, unless you know something against Ward Anders that maybe you should share with us."

Sam shrugged. "Don't know nothing against the man. I'm sure he'd be a great catch for some woman. Don't know how he'd be for one with any backbone, though." Looking as if he was suddenly bored with this conversation, he crossed the room in long strides and lifted his coat from one of the pegs by the door. "I'm going home," he announced, pulling it on.

Home, Sarah knew, was the foreman's house her grandfather had built for Ruth and Orville when they'd married. It was only about a hundred yards from the main house. Definitely not far enough, she thought.

"Dinner's at six," Ruth said as he grabbed another sandwich from the table before leaving.

"I'll just come by and get a plate to take back to my place," he replied. "I'm sure Sarah would like some time alone with you and Orville."

Before Ruth could respond, he was gone. Turning back to Sarah, she sighed heavily. "I've never understood why you and Sam never got along."

"He's the one who always needled me first," Sarah pointed out in her defense.

"I know," Ruth replied, turning to frown at the door Sam had exited through.

As Sarah swallowed another bite of sandwich, the thought of a hot bath filled her mind. "I'm going to go clean up," she said, already on her way out of the kitchen.

A few minutes later, as she lay soaking in the tub of hot water, Sam's image entered her mind uninvited. She shoved it out. His advice was the last thing she needed. She was a mature woman. She could think for herself.

Closing her eyes, she pictured Ward as she'd last seen him. He'd been twenty at the time, blond, athletic, with the clearest blue eyes she'd ever seen. His family was the wealthiest in town and rumored to be one of the wealthiest in the state. He'd been captain of the football team and president of his senior class.

Being the same age as Sam, Ward had graduated from high school two years ahead of her and gone away to college. Like nearly every other girl in town, she'd noticed him but she'd never dreamed she'd ever have a chance with him. Then the first Christmas vacation he was home, they'd worked together at a church social. The next day, he'd asked her out on a date. She'd been so flattered, she'd barely been able to speak.

After that they'd dated whenever he was home. The next summer, she'd had to go stay with her brother, Lester, and help him care for his young daughter. Ward had written often and when she'd returned home, he'd suggested they go steady. Putting her foolish reaction to Sam's kiss out of her mind, she'd agreed.

"But I was too bullheaded in those days," she muttered under her breath. "And insecure," she added. Choosing not to recall the more painful memories, she busied herself by washing her hair.

Old insecurities die hard, Sarah mused. It was the evening of the next day and Ward would be arriving to pick her up soon.

She'd spent the day visiting with Ruth and helping nurse Orville. He was feeling a little better and wanted to get up, but between her and her aunt they'd bullied him into staying in bed.

To her relief, Sam had kept his distance.

She'd guessed last night that, while he maintained a separate residence, he usually ate his meals with her aunt and uncle. Ruth had always been in charge of seeing that the hands were kept fed during the round-ups. And, considering the way her aunt felt about Sam, Sarah was sure Ruth was determined to see that he ate right. She knew she'd guessed correctly when she'd come down to breakfast this morning and found him there. But he'd finished quickly and left.

At lunchtime, he'd taken his meal in to Orville's room and talked to him about ranch business while he ate.

"Why in the world I'm even giving Sam Raven another moment's thought is beyond me," she snorted at her image in the mirror and returned her attention to her clothing. She'd changed three times before finally settling on the pale pink wool suit she now wore. Unless Ward had changed, he preferred elegant, dignified apparel. Never jeans and a sweatshirt even for a movie, she recalled.

Once again she inspected her image in the mirror. The cranberry silk blouse accented her ivory skin. A touch of charcoal eyeliner, in addition to her carefully applied mascara and eye shadow, emphasized her gray eyes. She'd gathered her hair, allowing the thick, straight tresses to drape loosely at the sides of her face, while in the back, she'd wound them into a chignon at her nape. The style gave a softness to her features while providing an air of calm dignity, she thought with approval.

The sudden worry that Ward's taste might have changed caused a sharp jab of uncertainty. But during lunch, when she'd asked Ruth about the Anders family, her aunt had informed her they were still the staunch pillars of society they'd always been. "When Ward, Senior, died, Ward stepped right into his father's shoes. And they fit him to a *T*," Ruth had finished.

Shaking off the small anxiety attack, Sarah added a pearl necklace and earrings as a final touch to her ensemble, then went downstairs.

Ruth smiled with approval as Sarah joined her in the kitchen. "You look lovely, dear."

Noticing Sam sitting at the table reading the newspaper, Sarah stiffened. Her nerves were tense enough without a final encounter with him just before Ward arrived. Maybe he would ignore her, she thought hopefully.

Her hopes plummeted as he peered over the top of the newspaper and his gaze traveled over her. His inspection was quick, taking only a couple of moments, but she felt it almost like a physical touch and had to fight to keep from squirming. Again she chided herself for reacting so strongly. It's simply my natural gut response bracing me to do battle, she reasoned.

"Looks like you'll fit in real well with the Anders," he said, completing his scrutiny and returning his attention to the article he'd been reading.

Sarah had the feeling he didn't consider that a compliment, but to her they were words of encouragement. "Thanks," she replied, then turning back to Ruth, returned her aunt's smile.

"Well, don't you look nice." Orville's voice sounded from behind her.

Glancing over her shoulder, Sarah saw her uncle entering the kitchen. He'd always been tall and lanky but now he looked much too thin to her. "You should still be in bed," she said with concern.

"I couldn't stand laying down any longer," he returned, seating himself at the table. "So I'm going to have my dinner sitting right here and then watch some television afterward. I'm getting too old to waste so much time sleeping."

Sarah touched his cheek. "Feels as if your fever is almost gone," she admitted. "But you should still take it easy."

"I'll make sure he does," Ruth replied, a look of purpose in her eyes.

Orville shook his head and gave Sam a conspiratorial wink. "Maybe you were right never to marry. That soft, sweet side of them is a thin layer. Inside they're as tough as steel and twice as unbendable."

Ruth placed her hands on her hips and glared at her husband. "Orville Perry!"

"'Course life without 'em would be downright dull," he added with a playful grin to let Ruth know he'd been teasing her.

Ruth shook her head, but behind her scowl Sarah saw a smile in her eyes. Again she experienced a twinge of envy.

As Ruth gave her stew a stir, she glanced over her shoulder at Sam. "Wouldn't do you no harm to give a look around for a wife. I ain't going to be here forever to cook for you."

"I can cook for myself when the need arises," he replied, and again turned his attention back to the newspaper.

"That'd sure be easier than finding a woman who'd be willing to put up with you," Sarah interjected, then mentally gulped when she realized she'd spoken aloud. She'd been hoping to avoid a confrontation with Sam tonight, but instead she was provoking one. Old habits die hard, she mused. Besides, the opportunity to give him a dose of his own medicine had been too tempting to pass up.

Sam looked up at her and cocked an eyebrow. "No one could ever accuse you of having a honey-coated tongue."

Orville shook his head. "Just like old times," he said, chuckling.

Ruth, however, didn't laugh as her gaze shifted between Sarah and Sam. "Both of you have as good a core as I've ever known two people to have. It's a shame your chemistries don't seem to blend well. I've always thought you would've made a good pair."

The image of herself married to Sam caused a curious curl of excitement in the pit of Sarah's stomach. Then she saw him give Ruth a look as if he thought she'd lost her mind and the curl turned to a cold lump.

The doorbell rang at that moment and, breathing a mental sigh of relief, Sarah bid the trio a good-evening and quickly hurried to greet Ward. She'd decided that with Sam in the kitchen with her aunt and uncle, she wouldn't encourage Ward to go in there and say hello. Instead she'd mention that Orville had the flu and it might be best if they merely left.

A slight prickling on the back of her neck distracted her momentarily. Attributing it to nerves, she ignored it as she braced herself for her first sight of Ward, then opened the door.

His boyishly handsome features had given way to a more mature countenance, she noted . . . a very handsome, statesmanlike one. He was wearing a long, heavy camel hair coat that prevented her seeing if his physique had changed much. However, the way he moved suggested he kept himself physically fit. His blond hair was still thick and cut in the same conservative style he'd worn as a young man. All in all, other than a few added age lines, he looked very much as she remembered him. Perhaps even a little more handsome, she thought and her nervousness increased.

"You look as lovely as ever," he said, entering and handing her a single red rose. The warmth left his smile as his gaze traveled past her. "Evening, Sam."

Startled, Sarah turned to see Sam leaning casually against the wall, his expression stoic as if he found the scene in front of him a bore. "Orville suggested you might not want to bring Ward into the kitchen and have him exposed to the flu," he said in an easy drawl.

Ruth suddenly entered the hall and flashed Sam an indignant scowl. "We don't mean to be unfriendly," she addressed Ward as she continued past Sam to come to a halt beside Sarah. "Orville and I just don't want anyone else getting sick." She smiled warmly. "As soon as Orville's well, you'll have to come for supper."

That should be a real treat, Sarah mused, picturing Sam tossing barbs her way all during the meal. Just his silent presence in the hallway was making her decidedly uncomfortable. "If we really don't want Ward exposed, then he and I should be going," she said. "Would you put this in water for me?" she added, handing the rose to her aunt.

The warmth had returned to Ward's smile. "You're looking as young as ever, Ruth. And I'll definitely take you up on that dinner invitation. I've heard your cooking is some of the best in the county."

He's still a charmer, Sarah thought, seeing her aunt blush with pleasure. Beyond Ruth's shoulder she saw

Sam give them all a dry look and head back into the kitchen. Good riddance! she thought. Retrieving her coat from the closet, she allowed Ward to help her put it on. Then bidding her aunt a good-night, she preceded him out the door.

Immediately he became the masculine protector, cautioning her to be careful and not slip. To make certain she didn't, he took hold of her arm. His cavalier manner was flattering and she remembered the first time he'd picked her up for a date. Excitement had bubbled through her. She'd expected to feel that same kind of wonderful exhilaration at this moment. Instead she merely continued to feel nervous. I'm too tense. Relax, she ordered herself, and smiled up at him as he helped her into his gray Mercedes.

He returned her smile with a warmth that brought a pleased flush to her cheeks. "Your taste in clothing has matured as exquisitely as you," he said with approval.

Recalling a time when he had not been so pleased with her choice of clothing, a sudden sour taste filled her mouth. Forget about the past, she ordered herself. She hadn't come here to make the same old mistakes. Hadn't she agonized over what to wear just so that she would please him? She should be delighted she'd succeeded. And she was, she assured herself, returning his smile.

"Rumbling Thunder's as hospitable as ever," he noted as they drove away.

The hint of ridicule in his voice when he'd used Sam's Indian name sent a curl of anger through Sarah. Startled by the urge to champion Sam, she reminded

herself that he had been less than friendly toward
Ward. Still she heard herself saying, "Sam's had a few
rough days lately."

They'd reached the end of the driveway. Stopped to
check for oncoming traffic before pulling out onto the
main road, Ward reached over and covered her hand
with his. "I was worried sick about you when I found
out you'd gone out in the storm." He glanced at her
and smiled warmly. "But then you always did add a
bit of excitement to my life."

Reading the heat in his eyes, Sarah again flushed
with pleasure. This was going well, she assured herself, and smiled back.

"I've thought a lot about you lately," Ward continued huskily. Reaching up he stroked her cheek in a
gentle caress, then returning his attention to the road,
pulled out and headed toward town.

The luxurious feel of the soft leather of his glove
lingered on Sarah's skin. "I've thought about you,
too," she admitted. A conciliatory note entered her
voice. "I was sorry to hear about Brenda's death."

"She was a good wife."

Sarah glanced at his profile. There had been a
kindness in his voice but no passion. He'd sounded,
she thought, as if he was talking about a deceased pet,
one who had served him well but was now gone and
nearly forgotten, instead of the woman to whom he
had been married for nearly eighteen years and who
had borne his children.

She was being much too critical. Brenda had been
gone more than two years now. It was healthy that he
was over his grief and ready to get on with his life.

Relax! she ordered herself once again. "Tell me about your children."

"Timothy is nineteen and in his first year at Harvard. He wants to be a lawyer," he replied, pride evident in his voice. "Jennifer is sixteen. She looks like her grandmother and has the same regal bearing as Miss Jocelyn."

Sarah's smile suddenly felt wooden. Everyone, including the members of Ward's family, referred to his mother as Miss Jocelyn. In some cases it was out of affection. In others, it was because she could intimidate with a glance and few people crossed her. And she liked being "Miss Jocelyn."

She'd once told Sarah that in this primitive, uncultured land, being addressed with respect was one of the few truly cultured dignities she had left. She never tired of reminding others that she'd been born and raised amid the upper crust of Charleston, South Carolina society. She expected to be treated with deference and she expected her wishes to be obeyed.

Wondering just how much Ward's daughter was like his mother, an uneasiness stirred within Sarah. She was an adult now, she reminded herself. Miss Jocelyn was not going to intimidate her and certainly no sixteen-year-old was, either.

"I hope you don't mind, I've arranged for us to have dinner at my home," Ward said, pulling her attention back to him. "There isn't a decent restaurant close by. Besides, my cook is excellent."

Sarah's smile became even more wooden. She forced an enthusiasm into her voice she didn't feel. "How wonderful. I'll get to meet your daughter."

"Regretfully, no," Ward replied with obvious disappointment evident in his voice. "She's away at boarding school. In fact, she's attending the same one my mother, Brenda's mother and Brenda attended. I do miss her, but she is among a better class of people there than she would be if I'd allowed her to attend school here."

Sarah recalled the time Ward had referred to her high school classmates as "the rabble masses." She'd taken offense, pointing out that she was one of those masses. He'd smiled that charming smile and informed her that she was most certainly a cut above the rest. At the time, she'd been flattered. Now his attitude caused a twinge of discomfort.

You're being too critical again, she chided herself. The man merely wants the best for his daughter and he can afford to give it to her. Besides, not having to face a younger version of Miss Jocelyn this evening would be a relief. "I'm sorry I won't get to meet her," she lied politely.

"You will in due time," he assured her. Reaching over, he again closed his hand around hers. "However, for this evening, I'm looking forward to having you to myself."

Sarah's smile became genuine once again. A romantic dinner for two, she mused, a sparkle glistening in her eyes.

This wasn't exactly how she'd envisioned their tête-à-tête, she was thinking a little later. They were seated in the formal dining room of Ward's home at a table that could easily seat a dozen people.

When they'd first entered the house, she'd had a sudden attack of worry that she would be overdressed for a simple dinner at home. Then Ward had taken off his coat and she'd seen that he was wearing a three-piece suit. Now seated here at his table, she felt confident in assuming that he continued his family's practice of dressing for dinner. Putting on nice clothes once a day wasn't such a bad notion, she'd told herself. She'd just need to increase her wardrobe a bit.

Ward occupied the head chair and she was immediately to his right. His butler had begun by presenting the wine, opening it, offering the cork first for Ward to sniff, then pouring a small amount in Ward's glass so that he could taste the deep red liquid to assure its quality. When this ritual had been completed, the wine approved and the glasses poured, the butler had stationed himself a few feet away, but with a clear view of the table. From there, with mostly hand signals and eye movements, he was directing the maid who was serving them their meal.

And Sarah felt herself under his watchful eye as well. That short assignment in England nursing a wealthy actress was paying off in added benefits, she thought. The first time she'd dined with Ward's family, she'd been totally intimidated by the array of dishes, glasses and silverware at her place setting. Now she knew exactly what the purpose of each was and when and how to use them. I've come a long way, she thought to herself. But not far enough, she added. While Ward seemed to easily ignore the presence of the others, she saw them as an audience.

And when the maid removed her soup bowl and then served the salad, she had to practically bite her tongue to keep from thanking the woman aloud. As she acknowledged the maid's service with a smile, her mind again flashed back to the first time she'd dined at Ward's home. As if Miss Jocelyn was there, Sarah could hear Ward's mother saying, "Sarah, dear, you mustn't thank the servants each time one of them performs a task. They do not expect it and it interrupts the flow of conversation. If you feel you must acknowledge their actions, then merely smile."

"Both mother and I were surprised when you chose a career in the military," Ward said, jerking her mind fully back to the present. "But when I learned they were going to put you through nursing school, I understood. You always did like taking care of people. I admired that in you."

A teasing expression came over his face and he lowered his voice conspiratorially. "Tell me the truth, did you ever try any of those Indian remedies Morning Dove taught you? I remember how excited you used to get when she'd take you herb hunting."

A flood of happy memories flowed through Sarah's mind. "I did try out a simple tealike brew she'd taught me on my commanding officer once when he had a particularly bad hangover. It got him into fit shape to face an inspection but for weeks he went around saying he wasn't sure which was worse, the hangover or the cure."

Ward joined in her light laughter and she actually did begin to relax.

"And did you see the world like the navy's ad promised?" he asked a few minutes later as their salad plates were being removed.

"Some," she replied. "And I've seen some since I retired."

He took her hand in his and gave it an encouraging squeeze. "Tell me about your travels. I want to know how your life has been since you left."

The honesty in his eyes caused a warmth to spread through her. As they ate, she told him about seeing Spain and England and about her tour of duty in the Far East.

"I thought we'd have dessert and coffee in the living room," he said as the dinner dishes were being cleared away.

"And you can tell me what you've been doing in your life," she suggested, feeling flattered but also self-conscious that he'd managed to keep the conversation centered on her during the entire meal.

"There's not much to tell," he replied, rising and shooing the butler back so that he could pull her chair out for her as if this was too great an honor for a mere servant. Then hooking his arm through hers, he guided her out of the dining room.

"After you left, I was emotionally at loose ends. Mother decided to take matters into her own hands. She called an old school friend who had a daughter a couple of years younger than I. That daughter turned out to be Brenda. I married her, graduated from college and went to work for my father," he said as they walked down the hall. "When he died, I took over the business. Brenda and I always got to Europe at least once a year. But mostly, I've lead a fairly quiet life. A great deal of my energy has been centered on making our bank one of the most solid in the state. And I do have some real estate interests that have kept me busy."

"You seem quite content," she noted. Of course, who wouldn't be, she added to herself. Beneath her feet was carpeting so thick she felt as if she was walking on a cloud. Luxury permeated the very atmosphere of this house and when Ward wanted to get away, he could go where he pleased.

They had reached the living room and releasing her arm, he took her hands in his. "I am content most of the time. But there are moments when I'm very lonely."

He was looking at her with desire in his eyes. Sarah's heart began to race. Although she'd envisioned this moment a hundred times, a part of her had never really expected it to happen. And certainly not this swiftly. Suddenly she didn't feel ready. Her gaze shifted past his shoulder. Immediately she stiffened. Hanging above the mantel over the fireplace was a portrait of his mother staring down at her.

Following the direction of her gaze, Ward glanced over his shoulder and grinned. "Very lifelike, isn't it?" he said, his voice carrying a strong note of admiration. "The artist captured the true essence of Miss Jocelyn."

"Definitely," Sarah admitted, feeling as if she was being scrutinized and not too kindly.

"I used to find Jennifer in here practicing that expression," he continued with a laugh. Then returning his attention to Sarah, he said apologetically, "I was moving too fast, wasn't I? It's just that the older I get the more rushed I feel to get on with my life. And now that I've seen you again, I can't help wondering why I ever let you go."

Sarah couldn't believe she wasn't melting into his arms. But instead, she heard herself saying, "That's very flattering."

To her relief a knock on the door interrupted them and the butler entered with a tray of cakes and coffee. Ward motioned the man to set the tray on the table by the fire, then instructed him that they would like to be left alone.

When the man had left, closing the door behind him, Ward again took Sarah by the arm and led her to the table. "My mother would like to see you again," he said as he seated her. "Would you consider having tea with her and me tomorrow?"

The thought of facing the woman in the portrait in the flesh sent a cold chill through Sarah, then her back straightened. If she was to have a future with Ward, she would have to learn to endure his mother. Besides, she again reminded herself, she was much more mature now. And most likely Miss Jocelyn wasn't nearly as intimidating as she remembered. "I'd love to have tea with you and your mother," she replied.

Ward beamed. "Good." Apology showed on his face. "I have a business lunch tomorrow I can't cancel. Would you mind meeting me at Mother's? She likes to take tea promptly at two."

"Two it is," Sarah confirmed.

"And she hates to see women wearing slacks at social functions," he added with a touch of self-
consciousness.

"I remember," Sarah replied.

His expression relaxed and she knew he expected her
to wear a dress or suit the next day. And she would.
After all, she had come back with the hope of finding
a peaceful, happy future for herself, not to stir up un-
necessary trouble. "Why don't you tell me about what
your mother has been doing to occupy her time during the past few years. That way, I'll be less likely to
bring up a subject that will strike a sore nerve. Knowing her interests will also give me topics for discussion."

Ward grinned. "You have learned diplomacy," he
said with approval.

The reference to her youthful shortcoming caused
Sarah to frown defensively. "I was never totally tact-
less. It's just that dealing with your mother requires a
great deal more patience than with most other people."

Immediately Ward's expression again became one
of apology. "I know, and I didn't mean to sound in-
sulting." His gaze warmed. "You've always been full
of fire. That was one of the qualities that drew me to
you. I'm simply happy to see that you have learned
how to control it. There is nothing so beautiful as a
fire under control nor anything so frightening as one
that is not."

She'd overreacted once again, Sarah admonished
herself. He was right. Learning to control one's emotions was part of maturing. She forced her jaw to re-

lax. "You were going to tell me about your mother's current interests."

Relief was visible on Ward's face. "Mother's still very proud of her garden, and both her home and garden were highlighted in a nationally distributed magazine a couple of years ago," he said, seating himself at the table as she poured them both coffee.

For the next hour Sarah felt as if she was being subtly tutored. Remembered sessions like this from their youth played through her mind. They were not her favorite memories. Again she fussed at herself for not being fair to him. He'd wanted her to make a good impression on his mother then and he wanted her to make a good impression on her now. And she could not fault him for that. If she and Ward were going to have a life together, their days would go much smoother if Miss Jocelyn approved of the match. Having had this little discussion with herself, she gave her full attention to what Ward was saying.

As he recounted what he obviously considered a humorous encounter between his mother and the mayor over the choice of flowers to be planted in the flower boxes on Main Street, Sarah found herself stifling a yawn.

"In the end, Miss Jocelyn had her way," Ward finished with a laugh. "Mayor Bradley could have saved himself from a few gray hairs if he'd just given in at the start."

Sarah forced a companionable grin.

Concern suddenly clouded Ward's features. "I'm boring you."

"It's been a long day," she hedged.

A gleam sparked in his eyes. "But not so long you won't honor me with one dance," he said coaxingly. Rising, he crossed the room and opened a maple cabinet to expose an elaborate stereo system. He pressed a button and a soft, slow melody filled the air. It was a recording that had been popular in their youth.

"This song was playing on the radio the first time I kissed you," he said.

"You remembered that?" Sarah asked in amazement, ashamed to admit she'd forgotten. But hearing the song again brought back the memories of excitement that first kiss had stirred and her smile again became genuine.

"I rarely forget the important moments of my life," he replied, taking her hand and gently pulling her to her feet. When she was standing, he stepped back and bowed, then straightened to face her. "May I have this dance?"

Sarah's smile broadened. Now this was more like what she'd hoped this evening would be like. "I'd be honored," she replied and slipped into his arms.

He had certainly kept himself in trim physical shape, she thought as they moved in unison to the moody rhythm. Pressed lightly against him, her cheek resting on his shoulder, she closed her eyes and breathed in the fragrant scent of his expensive aftershave. The imprint of his hand on her back was warm and pleasing. And she was aware of the smooth texture of the palm of his hand holding hers. Totally giving in to the moment, she forced everything but him and the music from her mind.

His hold tightened, drawing her more firmly against him. The sturdiness of his physique caused her blood to race. The music stopped, but he continued to hold her and her heart pounded wildly. Releasing her hand, he placed a finger under her chin and tilted her face upward.

She knew he was going to kiss her and she waited nervously. His lips were warm, she noted, as his mouth found hers. When she did not resist, he hardened the contact.

Sarah wove her fingers into his hair and added her own strength to the kiss.

His hand on her back moved lower. But instead of the erotic stimulation she expected to feel, her muscles tensed painfully. Relax, go with the moment, she ordered herself, but her body refused to obey. Gently she eased herself away from him. "I really think we should go, at least, a little more slowly."

"I just find it very difficult to keep my distance," he apologized, releasing her unhurriedly as if savoring each moment of the contact.

The adoration in his gaze caused her to again flush with pleasure. "You do know how to make a woman feel attractive."

"You," he said, "are delectable."

"You're making me feel like dessert," she bantered playfully.

"I'd like for you to be my dessert," he admitted. Regret showed on his face. "However, I will bow to your request and attempt to behave myself."

The hint in his voice that his good behavior was not a guarantee made her edgy. I suppose even fantasies require a little getting used to, she reasoned, unable to understand her reticence but unable to push it aside. Putting an inflection into her voice that suggested she wasn't totally sure her resolve would hold against another amorous assault, she said, "I really think it's time for me to be going home."

The hint of possible surrender brought a gleam of masculine triumph to his eyes and he leaned down to kiss her once again. But she eased away from him, letting him know she was serious about leaving.

He breathed a resigned sigh. "You win," he said, placing a light kiss on the tip of her nose, then gesturing toward the door.

Riding home, Sarah stared out at the star-filled sky. She'd been acting when she'd subtly implied that she was in danger of falling under the spell of his passionate overtures. His kiss had certainly been pleasant. But the bells and whistles she'd hoped for hadn't materialized.

Maybe I've grown too old for such unbridled passion, she thought. She studied Ward's profile. He was even more handsome than she'd expected and certainly more romantic. She should be bubbling with excitement.

"I'm so very glad you've come back," he said, breaking the silence between them.

In spite of the mixed emotions she was feeling, she heard herself saying honestly, "I am, too." But it wasn't Ward she was thinking about. Her gaze was again on the snow-covered landscape illuminated by moonlight. "I had forgotten how beautiful this land was."

"I hope that means you're seriously considering staying this time."

"I am," she replied.

A satisfied smile spread over his face as he drove on.

At the front door, he again kissed her. She tried to concentrate on the warmth of his lips, but the cold breeze whisking around them was chilling her.

"Tomorrow for tea at two sharp," he reminded her as she opened the door and started to go inside.

"Tomorrow at two sharp," she confirmed over her shoulder. Then bidding him a final good-night, she stepped inside. Trying hard to recapture the romantic sentiments of her youth, she stood at the window watching until he'd turned his car around and waved a last goodbye before heading back to the main road. But all she continued to feel was tense.

As she hung up her coat, the beginning of a headache caused her to grimace with pain. She dug out the bottle of aspirin from her purse then headed for the kitchen to get a glass of water. A light showed from under the door and she guessed Ruth had left it on for her. But as she entered the room, she was surprised to see Orville seated by the potbellied stove in the corner whittling. A fire was burning in the stove radiating a toasty warmth to ward off the chill of the night.

"I guess I got too much sleep the past few days. Didn't want to keep Ruth awake by lying there tossing and turning so I came in here for a while," he said in response to the surprised expression on her face.

"Are you honestly feeling better?" she asked solicitously.

"Better than you, it seems," he replied, cocking an eye at the aspirin bottle in her hand. Worry suddenly caused the already deep lines in his weatherworn face to deepen further. "I sure hope you haven't caught the bug from me."

Sarah shook her head. "No, it's just a headache."

"Date didn't go as good as you'd hoped?" he asked sympathetically.

Sarah swallowed the pills. Then, leaning against the counter, she frowned thoughtfully. "Actually it went much better than I expected."

Orville raised a skeptical eyebrow and she smiled sheepishly. "I'm just a little tense. I've spent a lot of time wondering what it would be like to see Ward again. I guess I'm still not used to the idea that it's really happening."

A knock on the back door caused her to jump slightly. Answering it, she found Sam there.

"Saw the lights on over here and thought I'd check to see if everything was all right," he said.

"Only trouble here is an old man who can't get to sleep," Orville replied, remaining seated and returning to his whittling. "Come on in and close that door before you let all the heat out."

Sarah expected Sam to refuse and go home, instead she was forced to quickly step back as he stepped forward. While she closed the door, he crossed over to the stove for a closer look at Orville and the concern for the old man she read on his face was proof yet again of how much he honestly cared for her uncle.

"Are you feeling worse?" he asked.

Orville gave him a disgruntled look. "I'm feeling just fine. If it wasn't for this damned arthritis in my knees and ankle, I'd get up and dance a jig for the both of you to prove it."

Sam's expression relaxed and he grinned. "Sounds like you're well on the road to recovery."

Sam did look handsome when he wasn't scowling, Sarah thought. Her headache suddenly increased and she began to massage her temple.

"Did your date go badly?"

She looked up to see Sam watching her. "No, it went very well, thank you," she replied.

His gaze shifted to the counter behind her where the aspirin bottle stood by the partially drunk glass of water. He raised an eyebrow, silently calling her a liar.

He probably thought she was too bullheaded and stubborn to behave like a demure lady through an entire evening, she thought acidly. Her back stiffened with defiance. "Ward wants to take up where we left off."

His expression remained skeptical as he continued to study her. "I'd think you'd be dancing around the room instead of swallowing aspirin," he observed.

The real reason for her tenseness suddenly occurred to her. "I'm having tea with Miss Jocelyn tomorrow."

Orville let out a chortle. "Now that'd give anyone a headache." He shook his head. "I don't like admitting it, but that woman scares me."

Sam had continued to keep his attention on Sarah. "So he's taking you home for Mama's inspection," he said dryly.

The way he'd spoken implied he thought Ward still felt the need for Miss Jocelyn's approval before choosing a wife. Sarah gave him a haughty look. "This is merely a courtesy call. She expressed a desire to see me so I'm going to see her. No sense in ruffling her feathers."

"She can make life downright unpleasant for those who do," Orville concurred with a snort.

As if suddenly bored by the conversation, the detached, aloof expression she was so used to seeing on Sam's face returned. "Seeing that everything's fine here, I'll be on my way," he said. At the door, he paused and looked back at Sarah. "Good luck tomorrow. I hope it works out well for you."

The honesty in his voice startled her. "Thanks," she managed to say as he strode out, pulling the door closed behind him.

Orville was banking the fire. "Guess we'd both better go get some rest," he said and Sarah nodded her agreement.

# Chapter Four

Turning into the wide semicircular driveway leading to Jocelyn Anders's home, Sarah felt her back muscles tightening. The house was a huge two-story affair reminiscent of the antebellum homes of the South. Balconies ran along both sides of the second floor while sturdy white columns holding up the two-story high porch roof stood like sentinels at the front of the house. A bit of Charleston elegance in the wilds of Wyoming, was how Miss Jocelyn described it.

"This is where all that confidence I learned in the military will really pay off," Sarah said aloud, her shoulders straightening with purpose.

She was wearing a silk pastel dress she had purchased in Paris. The pinks, greens and blues in the fabric were blended in a watercolor-washed design producing a softly flowing effect. The pale green heels

that matched the purse she was carrying were lying on
the seat beside her. In deference to the weather, at the
moment a pair of dressy boots adorned her feet. Her
hair was pulled back into a neat chignon at her nape
and she'd taken great pains with her makeup.

"Makeup should enhance without being flagrantly
noticeable," she repeated a well-remembered phrase
Miss Jocelyn had been fond of using. This was gen-
erally said, Sarah recalled, while the woman was
looking down her nose at the offender. Well, she
would give Miss Jocelyn no reason to criticize her today.

Ahead, parked on the circular driveway fronting the
house, she saw Ward's Mercedes. He climbed out as
she drove up and parked behind him.

Surprise registered on his face. "Did your car break
down?" he asked as he opened the door for her.

"No. This is my current mode of transportation,"
she replied, feeling the same curl of pride she'd felt
when she'd purchased the red pickup.

"It's a truck." A sharp edge in his voice suggested
he didn't think of that as an appropriate vehicle for a
woman to be driving.

Her pride of ownership dimmed. "It might not be
the most ladylike choice but it has proven to be the
most practical," she returned defensively.

His expression abruptly relaxed. "You always did
add that extra little spark to life," he said, smiling
charmingly.

The warmth in his eyes vanquished her defensive-
ness. Noting that the driveway and walkway had been
cleared of snow, she quickly pulled off her boots and

slipped on the green high heels. Then, climbing down from the cab, she smiled back as she accepted his arm and allowed him to escort her up the walk.

Out of the corner of her eye, she saw a curtain move slightly in the front room to her left. Intuitively she was sure Miss Jocelyn had been covertly watching her arrival. As if she were a soldier preparing to do battle, she braced herself as they entered the house.

"Miss Jocelyn is awaiting you in the front parlor," the butler informed her and Ward as he took their coats.

Mentally Sarah congratulated herself for guessing correctly about the person who was surreptitiously peering out at them.

"Thank you, Charles," Ward replied, and slipped his arm through Sarah's, guiding her across the wide entrance hall and into the room in which she'd seen the curtains flutter.

Miss Jocelyn had not changed a great deal in twenty years, Sarah thought. She was in stature a small woman, standing barely five feet three inches in height and weighing no more than a hundred and fifteen pounds. But Sarah had seen her stare down men a foot taller and three times her bulk. Granted, Miss Jocelyn's hair was now completely white and there were a few more lines around her eyes, but both only seemed to add to her regal bearing.

As Miss Jocelyn's gaze traveled appraisingly over her, Sarah was glad she'd given in to the frivolous impulse that had led her to purchase the extravagantly expensive Paris fashions. She knew Miss Jocelyn's own wardrobe came from the best houses and was fairly certain the woman could spot well-made clothing at a glance. And, unlike in her younger days, Sarah did not shirk under the woman's inspection but maintained the military bearing her years in the service had taught her.

"You do seem to have cleaned up nicely," Miss Jocelyn announced as she finished her scrutiny.

Ward scowled. "Mother, really!"

Miss Jocelyn lifted one shoulder in an elegant shrug. "I've always spoken my mind. I'm too old to change now."

Sarah had expected the inspection and felt a sense of pride at having passed muster. But deep inside, she could not help being piqued that Miss Jocelyn felt she had the right to pass judgment on others. Of course, Sarah was forced to admit in fairness, everyone had allowed Miss Jocelyn to do just that for so many years, one could not blame the woman entirely for having such a strong air of superiority.

However, Sarah was not quite willing to merely stand by idly and take any shots the woman might fire. Recalling that Miss Jocelyn did not enjoy anyone other than herself referring to her advancing age, she said politely, "The years seem to have been very good to you as well."

Ward's hand on Sarah's arm tightened and, glancing toward him, she saw the warning in his eyes. Mentally she scolded herself. She hadn't come here to rekindle an old conflict with his mother. She'd come here to set a truce.

"Yes, they have," Miss Jocelyn returned coolly. She motioned toward the table set in front of the fireplace. "Shall we be seated."

Ward hurried to help his mother into her chair.

Sarah started to seat herself then caught Miss Jocelyn watching her out of the corner of her eye and stopped. She waited until Ward had finished with his mother and then allowed him to seat her. Approval showed in Ward's smile and she congratulated herself for recalling this small bit of etiquette.

"I didn't know Orville had purchased a new truck," Miss Jocelyn remarked as she poured the tea. "And I'm especially surprised to see you driving it. But I suppose it was the safest vehicle for you to use to get into town. I understand a great many of the outer roads are still icy and snow covered."

Recalling Ward's reaction, Sarah was momentarily tempted to allow this misconception to stand. But pride would not allow that. "It's my truck," she said.

Miss Jocelyn set the teapot down and looked at her. "Cowgirls own trucks. Ladies do not."

Ward frowned reprovingly at his mother. "A truck is a very practical vehicle. I'm sure Sarah had a good reason for purchasing it."

In all honesty, Sarah had to admit that the purchase of the truck had been another of her more impulsive acts rather than a carefully thought-out buy. But very soon afterward it had proved to be a practical decision. However, she was in no mood to justify her actions to Miss Jocelyn, so she merely smiled and remained silent.

Miss Jocelyn gave her son a haughty glare but allowed the subject to drop as she offered tea cakes.

Sarah tried to convince herself that she should be pleased that Ward had come to her defense. But she couldn't shake the disquieting effect that knowing down deep he, too, disapproved of her owning a truck was causing. Maybe he's afraid I'll start chewing tobacco next, she mused, then had to fight the urge to giggle. Realizing her close brush with laughter was more a sign of nervousness than amusement, she again ordered herself to relax.

"My son has informed me that seeing you again has rekindled the fires of his youth. And he is interested in courting you with the possibility of marriage as an outcome."

Sarah, who had been lifting a tea cake to her plate, nearly dropped it. That is what you wanted, she reminded herself. She just hadn't expected Ward to be so candid with his mother, nor to have Miss Jocelyn repeating his words so bluntly.

"He tells me that you've learned how to dress properly and you've traveled extensively thus broadening your horizons. And I can see that your manners have improved tremendously," Miss Jocelyn continued.

Sarah suddenly found herself wondering if she'd be sitting there having tea if she hadn't dressed properly or known which utensil to use at dinner the previous evening. Her gaze shifted to Ward. He was looking quite pleased with himself.

"I know you think I'm being precipitous but you positively astonished me last night," he said. "I will admit that although I could not resist seeing you again, I had my doubts that we could have a life together. Now I know that we can. You would fit perfectly into my world." He grinned impishly. "You can even keep your truck."

Although Ward obviously felt a lustiness toward her, it was not as important to him as her manners and dress! And love had not even been mentioned. Sarah began to feel claustrophobic. "I don't know what to say," she choked out.

Miss Jocelyn raised a hand like a policeman halting traffic. "There is just one other little question that has to be asked before this goes any further." Her gaze narrowed on Sarah. "We Anders have a reputation to uphold. As far as I have been able to discern through the years, your family has no real skeletons in the closet. However, there is a question of what you have been doing these past twenty or so years. If there is any scandalous behavior in which you have participated that could bring embarrassment to me or my son, I feel it's only fair for you to tell us now."

Sarah stared at the woman for a long moment as a silence descended over the room. Then, realizing that Ward had said nothing, she turned to him. He looked as if he was actually waiting for her to respond. Sarah's jaw tightened with self-righteous indignation.

"I'm sure Sarah has done nothing to embarrass herself or us," he spoke up quickly, obviously reading the angered pride on her face.

Sarah felt like a fool. How could she have been such an idiot! An impish urge she could not resist bubbled to the surface. "Of course not," she replied with cool dignity. "Unless you consider skinny-dipping with a marine regiment." She screwed her face up into a thoughtful grimace. "And I do think someone took home videos."

Both Ward and Miss Jocelyn paled.

Sarah grinned. "Just kidding."

Ward scowled. "Jokes like that can be dangerous. You know how rumors fly around this town."

"Your sense of humor does not seem to have matured along with the rest of you," Miss Jocelyn observed.

"You're right," Sarah agreed. "And I don't think I will fit very well into your family." She rose from the table. "I believe I'll be on my way."

She was not surprised when Ward did not try to stop her. Furious with herself for not having faced the truth long ago, she thanked the butler as he helped her on with her coat, then she strode out of the house. Reaching her truck, she gave it a loving pat.

Relief spread through her as she drove away. She'd never have been happy in Ward's world. Just the thought of more afternoon teas with Miss Jocelyn caused her stomach to knot. And then there was Ward's daughter. Having a duplicate of Miss Jocelyn home for the holidays could really put a damper on the festivities.

"Guess it's going to be just me and my truck," she muttered, pulling over to the side of the road a couple of blocks from Miss Jocelyn's house and changing back into her boots. As the full realization of what had happened sank in, a sense of intense loneliness swept through her. Still she had no regrets about bidding

Ward goodbye. "That would have been a match made in hell," she admitted. She was looking for someone to love and be loved by and he was looking for someone who knew which fork to use.

Returning to the ranch, Sarah continued around to the back of the main house to park. As soon as she rounded the corner, she groaned. Sam was there splitting wood. He was the last person she wanted to face right now.

"You're home early," he said, leaning on his ax and watching her climb down from the cab.

She gave a nonchalant shrug. "Ward's a snob."

He regarded her dryly. "You're just now finding that out?"

"So I got my head turned by a handsome face," she shot back. "Men are always falling for women with looks but no substance."

"True," he conceded.

Deciding not to wait for the sarcastic barb she was sure he would send her way at any moment, she started into the house.

"Are you all right?" he asked unexpectedly.

Startled by the honest concern she heard in his voice, she turned back. He was watching her with an unreadable expression on his face. "I'm fine," she replied.

He continued to regard her stoically. "I'm sorry things didn't work out the way you wanted them to."

Embarrassment suddenly brought a flush to her cheeks. He was feeling sorry for her! "I don't need your pity!" she snapped.

"You don't have it. By my reckoning, you've just escaped a fate worse than death."

A corner of her mouth curled up into a crooked grin. "I think you're right."

He nodded as if to say he knew he was, then turned his attention back to the woodpile.

Ruth was standing at the door to greet her by the time Sarah reached the porch. "I didn't expect you back so soon. Was Miss Jocelyn in a particularly vicious mood today?" she asked solicitously as Sarah entered the kitchen and began taking off her coat. The motherly protectiveness on her face increased. "If so, you should put her out of your mind and just think about Ward."

"They're cut from the same cloth," Sarah said bluntly.

Ruth frowned. "I was afraid of that but, for your sake, I hoped I was wrong." She waved toward the table. "You sit down and I'll pour you a cup of coffee to warm you. You look chilled."

"I feel like a fool who tried to recapture something that was never there in the first place," Sarah admitted as she sat down. "I guess I was just grabbing at straws. I've never found Mr. Right and I wanted to. So I figured that maybe I'd left him behind."

"A girl's first romance can have a strong hold on her," Ruth said, setting two cups of coffee on the table and seating herself across from Sarah.

Sarah sighed heavily. "These past years, I've been blaming my own immaturity for Ward's and my original breakup. Fairly soon after we started dating, he began to make suggestions about what I should wear.

He also began instructing me on my manners. He said
this was simply because he wanted me to feel comfortable when I was with his family, and I could see his
point. Miss Jocelyn has a very narrow spectrum of
tolerance. But a part of me rebelled. I accused him of
having a Pygmalion complex and of not being willing
to accept me as I was. He replied that he was simply
helping me improve myself. I was hurt and told him
that if he couldn't accept me the way I was then we
were through. He said I was being bullheaded.''

"And so you ran off and joined the navy," Ruth
finished the explanation for her.

"And so I ran off and joined the navy," Sarah confirmed. "Clearly my instincts knew what was right for
me.''

Reaching across the table, Ruth took Sarah's hand
and gave it a squeeze. "I do hope this business with
Ward isn't going to cause you to go packing immediately. I was hoping for a nice long visit. Winters can
get real lonesome here.''

Sarah saw the plea in her aunt's eyes. "I'll stick
around for a while," she promised.

Ruth smiled brightly. "Good.''

A kick on the back door caused both of them to
jump. "It's Sam with wood," Ruth said, getting up
and letting him in. Then tossing a final smile at Sarah,
she added, "I'm going to go check on Orville. He was
doing some bookkeeping but it's my guess he's
stretched out on the couch sleeping. And I may take a
little nap myself before starting dinner.''

As Ruth left Sarah alone with Sam, Sarah's nerves
tensed. She lowered her gaze to her coffee but still she

was aware of his boot steps as he crossed the room. I don't understand why I let that man's presence unsettle me so easily, she fumed. But it did. "I'm going to change into something more comfortable," she announced abruptly. Immediately she felt like a fool. She was behaving as if she needed an excuse to escape.

But she didn't, she mocked herself as she looked in Sam's direction. He was unloading the wood, seemingly totally oblivious to her presence. Jerking her gaze away from him, she started toward the door.

"I noticed you're traveling pretty heavy," he said in an easy drawl before she'd taken two steps.

Coming to a halt, she turned and frowned at him in confusion.

"Couldn't help seeing you've got the back of your truck packed pretty full," he elaborated.

"I was going to rent my house in California but the young couple who came to see it wanted to buy it so I sold it to them." She expected to feel at least a prick of regret at what now could be considered an unwise decision. But she felt none. She gave a shrug. "It was just a place to hang my hat between assignments. The past couple of years, I've been gone more than I've been there. Everything I wanted to keep is now in the back of my truck. Lucky for me, I'd purchased a vehicle large enough to haul all of it."

He smiled smugly as if she'd just confirmed a suspicion he'd had. "You have the spirit of a wanderer."

"I prefer to think of myself as a searcher looking for the place where I will be the most happy," she flung back and strode from the room.

But as she changed into jeans and a sweatshirt, she had to admit that it bothered her that she had not yet found a place where she felt so comfortable she wanted to stay. "Well, at least no one can accuse me of living in a rut," she observed in an attempt to lighten her mood. Instead the hollowness that had brought her here grew more intense. Quickly putting on a pair of sneakers, she went downstairs.

Her first stop was the study. There she found Orville asleep on the couch just as Ruth had predicted. Approaching him, she noted his breathing was regular and his face did not look flushed. Relieved that he was recovering nicely, she left him and went into the kitchen. Too tense to simply sit and wait for Ruth to join her so they could cook dinner, she gathered the ingredients to make dinner rolls. She was kneading the remainder of the flour into the dough when Sam entered.

"Afternoon," he said.

She'd expected him to go about his business without even acknowledging her. Glancing up, she saw him approaching the table where she was working. The tenseness that mixing the bread had helped ease came back full force. "Afternoon," she replied, and returned her attention to her dough.

"Do you still cook as inventively as you used to?"

She looked up at him, certain she would see ridicule on his face; instead there was stiff politeness. "If you're wondering if I'm planning to add a few herbs to these dinner rolls in their final preparation, then the answer is yes," she said. "I believed Morning Dove when she told me that root plants and herbs are healthy. Besides, I like the added flavor. However, if you prefer your food plain, I'll set aside a few."

"There's no need for that. I enjoy a little added potency to my food as well," he replied. His jaw hardened with purpose. "I was wondering if I could have a few words in private with you."

Surprised by this request, she glanced over her shoulder to see if anyone had entered the room. They hadn't. She turned back to him. "I thought we were having a private conversation."

He frowned impatiently. "I would prefer someplace where I don't have to worry about us being interrupted. Would you mind coming over to my place?"

Sarah, who had returned her attention to her dough, froze in midmotion. He'd invited her to his home. Those were words she'd never expected to hear. Again looking up at him, she saw the hard set of his jaw. What in the world could he want to talk to her about that was so private? she wondered. Suddenly the thought that either Orville or Ruth was more ill than they wanted anyone in the family to know and Sam felt it was his duty to let someone in on the secret occurred to her. "I'll be over in a minute or two," she promised.

Sam acknowledged her reply with a nod and left.

Deeply worried about Ruth and Orville, she quickly finished with the dough and put it in a bowl to rise. Washing her hands but leaving her work area to be cleaned up later, she grabbed her coat from the peg, pulled it on and dashed across to the foreman's residence.

Sam opened the door for her as she reached his porch. Stepping inside she was surprised by how comfortable the interior felt. She'd expected it to be cold and uninviting. Granted the decor was decidedly masculine, still there was a cozy air about the place. Startled that she would think of anything in regard to Sam as "cozy," she pushed her thoughts about her surroundings to the back of her mind and faced him levelly. "Is Ruth or Orville more ill than they have led me to believe?" she asked anxiously.

"No. They're both just getting on in years," he replied.

Sarah breathed a sigh of relief. "I'm glad to hear that." Her anxiousness for her aunt and uncle now gone, she frowned in confusion. "Then what did you want to talk to me about?"

His shoulders squared. "I want to purchase some of your time."

Her confusion increased. "You look perfectly healthy to me." Amazingly healthy, she added to herself, thinking that she'd never seen a man who looked more fit.

"Not as a nurse but as my wife," he stated bluntly.

For a long moment Sarah's vocal cords refused to work and all she could do was stare. A flush of anger burned her cheeks as her voice returned. "I really don't sell that kind of service," she snapped, and started toward the door.

"Wait, please." He blocked her path. "That didn't come out exactly right."

"It sounded pretty clear to me," she returned dryly. But beneath the cool surface she was presenting, she was feeling decidedly shaken. To her chagrin, instead of labeling his offer as preposterous, she found herself wondering what being his wife would be like. It'd be like living in a constant war zone, she answered her own question.

"You'd be my wife in name only."

The thought that that didn't sound like the least bit of fun, flashed through her mind. Startled by this wanton reaction, she simply regarded him mutely and waited for him to continue.

"I want to buy this ranch. And Orville and Ruth would like to sell it to me. Orville needs to be in a warmer climate. I'm sure you've noticed his arthritis is pretty bad, and with each winter it gets worse. The doctor says he'd be more comfortable if he was to move to Arizona or New Mexico. But Orville made a deathbed promise to your grandfather that he would keep this ranch in the Perry family. And even though there isn't anyone in the family who's interested in purchasing this place or even keeping it once Orville and Ruth are gone, Orville feels honor-bound to hold on to it."

Sarah saw the light. "But if you were married to me that might make him feel you were enough a part of the family to allow his conscience to let you purchase the place," she concluded for him.

Sam nodded. "That's about it."

"My cup runneth over," Sarah muttered sarcastically. "One man is interested in me because I know how to dress and which utensil to use at a formally set table and another wants to marry me so he can purchase a ranch. What more could a girl ask for?"

Sam frowned. "I'm merely asking for a little of your time and you'd be doing Ruth and Orville a favor."

"I'll think about it." She couldn't believe she'd actually agreed to consider his proposition. What was even more unnerving was that she discovered herself seriously considering accepting. She was simply concerned about Orville and Ruth, she reasoned, attempting to understand this unexpected reaction.

"Thanks," he said.

Her mouth too dry to respond, she merely nodded and left.

"What in the world were you doing outside?" Ruth asked as Sarah entered the kitchen through the back door. "I assumed you were up in your room."

"I just went out for a breath of fresh air," Sarah lied, glad to be inside. The distance she'd had to traverse from Sam's place to the main house had not been long but the icy breeze that had fought her all the way had chilled her to the bone. She thought about Orville and knew that kind of cold had to be making his arthritis terribly painful.

"Looks like you nearly froze yourself," Ruth observed.

"It was colder out there than I thought," Sarah admitted, hanging her coat on one of the pegs near the door. The heat radiating from the potbellied stove beckoned her. Approaching the stove, she held her hands out to defrost them.

Joining her, Ruth extended a cup of coffee to her. "You look like you could use some warming up."

"Thanks." Sarah accepted the hot brew gratefully.

Settling herself into one of the rocking chairs beside the fire, Ruth motioned for Sarah to seat herself in the other. "I see you've got some dough rising."

Sarah nodded. "It's for dinner rolls. Thought I'd add some herbs to give them a little extra flavor. I can leave some plain, though, if you'd prefer."

Ruth grinned. "Probably be good for Orville and me to add a little more spice to our lives."

As Sarah took a sip of coffee, she studied her aunt over the brim of her cup while Sam's proposal again played through her mind. "Have you and Orville ever considered moving to a warmer climate?" she asked, keeping her voice casual.

A wistful expression spread over Ruth's face. "Fact is, the doctor has suggested a change of climate might be good for Orville. My sister, Abigail, and her husband live in Arizona and we go visit them for a while every winter. Orville does seem to be more comfortable while we're there and he gets along real well with both my sister and her husband. Truth is, the four of us have a real nice time together."

Clearly Ruth did want to move and it sounded as if Orville would not object, Sarah concluded. Deciding to probe further, she said, "Maybe you should consider selling this place and moving."

"We'd like to do just that," Ruth admitted frankly. "More to the point, we'd like to sell it to Sam. He wants it and he deserves to have it. There's been a few tough years when we could barely make ends meet. There wasn't even enough money to pay Sam his salary. It probably would have killed Orville to keep this place going by himself. But he didn't have to. Sam stayed just for room and board. This ranch has been home to me and Orville but we've never loved it the way your Grandpa Perry did."

Ruth sighed heavily. "Sam, now he loves this land like your granddaddy did. But your Grandpa Perry made Orville make him a deathbed promise to keep this ranch in the Perry family." Ruth shook her head as regret showed on her face. "It don't seem fair to us or Sam, but that's the way it is."

Sam had assessed the situation honestly, Sarah had to admit. But there was still one more question that needed an answer. "If Sam was married to someone with Perry blood, me for instance, would that qualify him as a buyer?" she asked, keeping her voice casual.

For a moment Ruth stared at her in stunned surprise, then said, "Of course it would." Her gaze narrowed on her niece. "Why would you ask that?"

Sarah shrugged. "I just wondered, that's all," she replied with an air of nonchalance.

For a moment Ruth looked as if she was going to probe further, then she clamped her mouth shut and sat covertly studying Sarah.

Sarah knew she was being watched but was too preoccupied with her own thoughts to care. Ever since Sam had made his proposal, a nervous excitement had been building inside of her. It was reminiscent of the time she'd gone skydiving on a dare. Again she told herself she was crazy but she found herself tempted to take him up on his offer.

She tried convincing herself this was strictly for selfless reasons... that she was concerned about Orville's health and wanted to aid her aunt and uncle. But the truth was, even if Ruth had implied that Orville might change his mind and not sell, she still would be tempted to go through with the wedding.

Grudgingly she admitted she had never been able to entirely forget that youthful kiss. Of course, there would be no kissing and no touching in this marriage, she reminded herself. Their union was to be more of a sham than a real marriage.

However, Sam had always been an enigma to her. This would, no doubt, be her only opportunity to discover what was behind that stoic mask from which he viewed the world most of the time. There was the possibility she might be disappointed by what she discovered, she cautioned herself. He could simply be basically cynical at his core.

Still, her curiosity was higher than it had ever been about anything before. And wasn't that her prerequisite for taking on any job? she asked herself. Hadn't she vowed that she would only seek out those assignments that offered a chance for adventure? Besides, she should do this for Orville and Ruth's sake, she told herself, completing her argument.

"You look like a woman with a purpose," Ruth said, breaking into Sarah's thoughts.

There was a question in Ruth's voice and Sarah looked up to see Ruth watching her worriedly. She smiled confidently. "I am. I'm going to check on my dough. I placed it in a warm spot so it would rise quickly."

But as she crossed the room and caught a glimpse of the foreman's house through the window, her confidence faltered. What harm could marrying Sam do? she chided herself. Even if he proved to be a complete bore, her time wouldn't be wasted. There was Ruth and Orville to consider. If she could help relocate them to a better climate, she would be happy.

She had lifted the cloth from her dough to discover it was rising nicely when a knock on the back door was followed by Sam's entrance. As she replaced the cloth, her hand trembled slightly. Let the adventure begin, she told herself, and turned to face him.

"Evening, Ruth," he said as he hung his coat on a peg.

"Evening," she replied. "Orville's in the den. Dinner will be a little bit late. I took a nap and I'm moving a mite slow."

Sarah immediately felt guilty for not having offered to cook the entire meal. "You just tell me what you were planning on fixing and I'll fix it," she said quickly.

"We'll fix it together," Ruth stated. "I don't mind help but I ain't ready to sit down and rock my life away."

As Ruth rose and started toward the refrigerator, instead of going on into the den, Sam turned to Sarah. "I brought you a peace offering." Approaching her, he extended a wood carving. "I figure it's time the two of us buried the hatchet."

Past his shoulder, Sarah saw Ruth jerk around and stare at them. Then Ruth was forgotten as she looked up into Sam's face. Deep in the dark brown depths of his eyes was a plea so intense it nearly took her breath away. Ruth had been right about how strongly Sam was attached to this ranch, she thought. Accepting the gift, her hand brushed against his. An unexpected current of heat raced up her arm and she quickly dropped her gaze to the wooden object she was holding.

It was a wolf and she was surprised by the intricate details of his work. "This is lovely," she said, examining it closer. Drawing a steadying breath, she met his gaze. "I accept your offer," she said in hushed tones. Then, for Ruth's benefit, she smiled brightly and said more loudly, "Thank you."

Relief showed in his eyes. "You're welcome."

Sarah expected a wave of panic. After all, she had just agreed to a marriage between herself and her lifelong nemesis. Instead the relief in his eyes sent a curl of pleasure through her.

"All right, you two," Ruth snapped. When both Sarah and Sam turned to her, expressions of innocence on their faces, she motioned toward the back door. "Sam's place, now!"

Walking over to the door, she began pulling on her coat. "Now!" she said when they continued to stand immobile.

Mentally Sarah groaned. Her questions had obviously aroused Ruth's suspicions. She and Sam could bluff their way through this, she assured herself. If not, she would never forgive herself. She'd just always been one of those people who had a need to double-check the facts. But in this case, that need had been foolish. Sam would never have considered suggesting a marriage between the two of them if he hadn't been one hundred percent certain his ploy would work.

She glanced up at him to discover the stoic expression had returned to his face. The thought that he would hate her forever if she ruined his plan brought a painful stab of regret. We've never gotten along, she reminded herself curtly. Animosity between us would simply be returning to status quo. It's really destroying Orville and Ruth's chance to sell this place that I will truly regret, she assured herself.

As soon as they were inside Sam's house, Ruth turned and faced them. "I want to know what's going on," she demanded. Her gaze leveled on Sarah. "My body may be past its prime but my mind's working first-class. First you ask me about whether your being married to Sam would qualify him to buy this ranch. Then he comes in and gives you a gift. Right then I braced myself for one heck of a battle. I figured Sam had been being nice to you and you were looking for a reason. And I was feeling real guilty for having given you that reason. I've always thought that if you two could spend a little friendly time together, you'd learn to get along."

The suspicion in Ruth's eyes deepened. "But I figured I'd ruined that chance. I expected you to throw his gift right back at him and tell him to find someone more gullible. Instead you were all smiles."

She turned to Sam. "Have you struck some kind of a deal with Sarah so you can purchase this ranch?"

Sam drew a harsh breath but before he could speak, Ruth held up her hand as a signal for silence. "No, wait, don't tell me anything," she said curtly. "I've never lied to Orville and I won't start now. If you two have worked out an agreement that is beneficial to both of you, then I'm glad. But you'd better make sure Orville believes this is a love match and you intend for it to last. As much as I want Sam to have this ranch, I couldn't bear to see Orville spend the rest of his days feeling as if he'd betrayed his father's trust."

"I wouldn't do anything to bring harm to either you or Orville," Sam vowed.

"Neither of us would," Sarah added.

Ruth regarded them in silence for a long moment, then nodded. "I'll take your words on that." Suddenly she grinned. "Winters around here are usually pretty dull. But watching the two of you should be real interesting." Still grinning, she started to the door. "But right now I have a dinner to cook."

"I'll be there in a minute," Sarah called after her. As the door closed behind Ruth, she turned to Sam. "I'm sorry. I almost blew it."

"Ruth's sharp. She would have suspected something anyway. This way we know we have her on our side." His gaze hardened and his shoulders straightened with pride. "I appreciate you helping me."

The depth of gratitude she saw on his face shook her. This ranch really was his life, she thought. A curl of envy twisted through her. Why couldn't she find a man who would care for her the way Sam cared for this ranch? "I'd better get back to the house and help Ruth," she said stiffly.

# Chapter Five

"**W**ell, this has got to have been the most interesting dinner I've sat through in quite awhile," Ruth said as she finished the last bite of her slice of apple pie. A mischievousness sparkled in her eyes as her gaze traveled from Sam to Sarah, then back to Sam. "It was real pleasant to hear the two of you conversing without throwing darts at each other."

Orville laughed. "Never thought I'd live to see the day."

Sarah saw the satisfaction on Ruth's face and realized her aunt's remark had been aimed at making certain Orville had noticed that Sarah and Sam were on more friendly ground. "We've decided to bury the hatchet," she said for extra emphasis.

"In the bosom of peace rather than in each other from now on," Sam added with a lopsided grin.

Sarah looked at him in surprise. "You made a joke." The moment the words were out, she wished she'd bitten her tongue. Out of the corner of her eye she saw that Ruth's smile had faded and in its place was an "I knew this peace wouldn't last" expression. But instead of the impatient scowl she expected to see spread over Sam's features, he merely grinned more crookedly.

"Sometimes I just can't stop myself and my sense of humor escapes," he said.

Startled to find his grin so infectious, Sarah grinned back. "I like it."

"Well, now," Orville mused thoughtfully. "You two do seem to be getting along right well. Might even be safe to leave you alone in a room together."

The thought of being alone with Sam caused excitement to stir within her. Then Sarah's mind flashed back to the cabin. He'd clearly disliked being cloistered there with her. And at this moment, he was merely putting on an act for Orville's benefit, she reminded herself, and the excitement died. "Looks like it's time to clear the table," she said, abruptly rising.

Out of the corner of her eye she saw Sam's stoic mask again descend over his features and guessed he was relieved that the meal was over.

"Your coming for a visit has definitely livened up my winter," Ruth remarked a little later as she washed the dinner dishes and Sarah dried.

"It's proven rather unexpected for me, too," Sarah admitted. She'd been trying not to think about Sam. She didn't doubt for even a moment that his only interest was in obtaining the ranch. And the momentary bursts of excitement she was experiencing when thinking about him were beginning to irritate her. To combat this irritation, she'd been concentrating on Orville and Ruth and again assuring herself that she was only going through with the marriage for their sake and because of a certain curiosity about what made Sam Raven tick. But curiosity was all it was, she assured herself.

Ruth's expression suddenly became serious. "I don't want you doing anything rash for Orville's and my sakes," she said sternly. "But you could use this opportunity to get to know Sam better. He's a good man. I know he's rough around the edges . . . well, actually, he's got a pretty thick, rough hide all-round. But inside he's got a soft heart."

Sarah guessed she would never get a glimpse of Sam's heart but she didn't tell Ruth that. Instead she forced a playful smile. "And a sense of humor," she added.

Ruth's smile returned. "That, too."

They had just finished the dishes when Sam and Orville came into the kitchen. "We've got all the records in order," Orville announced, seating himself in one of the rocking chairs by the fire. "This winter's a tough one but the stock's holding up."

Sarah heard the tiredness in his voice. He deserved a few years to bask in the sun and take life easy. Both he and Ruth did. Mentally she groaned. Why did she feel she had to keep justifying her decision to aid Sam? Because a part of me thinks I'm a brick or two short of a full load to be considering marrying the man, came the answer.

But she knew that wasn't quite true. What Sam had proposed was a business arrangement. What really had her unnerved was that she honestly wanted to spend time with him.

It was merely an old curiosity, she assured herself for the umpteenth time. Sam was a mystery she had a need to understand better. What she didn't understand was why the need was so strong.

"I'm thinking of driving into Rawlins tomorrow," Sam announced as he pulled on his coat. "I was wondering if you'd like to ride along, Sarah. We could go to a matinee, then stop somewhere for dinner on the way home."

"Sure," she replied nonchalantly. But she didn't feel nonchalant. What she felt like was a teenager being asked on her first date. I just never expected to hear those words coming from his mouth, she reasoned.

"Good." He smiled stiffly. "We'll leave right after breakfast." Nodding goodbye to Ruth and Orville, he left.

"Well, will miracles never cease." Orville chuckled. He shook his head in disbelief. "Sarah and Sam on a date."

"Miracles, indeed," Ruth agreed.

But Sarah saw the hint of guilt behind Ruth's smile. "I'm sure I'll have an interesting day," she said. Then for Ruth's sake, she forced a mischievous grin and added, "It's an opportunity I wouldn't want to pass up."

The edge of guilt faded, and Ruth's smile became more relaxed.

But later lying in bed, staring into the dark, Sarah's nerves were so tense she could feel them tingling. He'd probably revert to his usual stoic self the moment they were away from Orville and Ruth, she told herself. More than likely, tomorrow would be one of the more boring days of her life.

Still, she could not relax. She pounded her pillow trying to get it into a comfortable shape. Nothing she did to it worked. Giving up, she tossed and turned restlessly until she finally fell asleep.

The next morning when her alarm woke her, Sarah nearly bolted out of bed. "I'm too old to be this anxious about a date that isn't even really a date but just an act," she growled at herself as she combed her hair and brushed her teeth.

Still, she took pains with her makeup. Then there was the decision about what to wear. She assumed casual attire would be appropriate. The only times she'd ever seen Sam in a suit was on Sundays and at her grandparents' funerals. But how causal? she wondered. Jeans? Slacks? A skirt? Her head started to pound. "I cannot believe I'm so worried about choosing the right outfit," she snarled at herself. Sam probably wouldn't even notice.

Her jaw firmed. "Slacks and a sweater," she said with determination, then grabbed a blue-and-white ensemble. In the next instant, she tossed them back and pulled out a flowery print skirt and a red blouse. "He's not even going to notice what I'm wearing," she told herself again as she traded the skirt and blouse for a pair of tan slacks and a pale pink sweater with tiny blue flowers embroidered on it.

Still scowling at herself, she dressed in the slacks and sweater then hurried downstairs to help Ruth with breakfast.

But as she entered the kitchen, her nervousness multiplied. Sam was already there. She'd hoped to have at least one cup of coffee to pull herself together before he arrived.

"You look real nice," he said, glancing up from the newspaper.

Although his tone was friendly, she noticed his gaze was cool. There were tired circles under his eyes as well. He looked like a man who had spent a long night reconsidering his actions. *And has concluded that this ranch isn't worth the struggle to be pleasant to me for an extended length of time,* she finished.

Her shoulders straightened with pride. *And I'm relieved not to have to go through this charade.* But she didn't feel relieved. She felt piqued. *I'm just sorry for Ruth and Orville,* she assured herself.

"Thanks," she replied to his greeting, keeping her tone neutral, then turned her attention to Ruth and bid her aunt a warm good-morning.

As she poured herself a cup of coffee, she studied Sam covertly. He was dressed in a pair of nearly new jeans and a blue cotton dress shirt. He even had on a string tie and his hair was tied back with a leather thong. Clearly he was dressed for a day in town. Still, she was certain he was going to break their date.

Abruptly, he set the newspaper aside and rose. "We'll leave in half an hour, if that's all right with you," he said, heading for the door.

She had to fight to hide her surprise. "That's fine with me," she managed to reply to his departing back as he grabbed his coat from its peg and continued on out.

"Sam's been acting like a man with something gnawing at him," Ruth said as she set a plate of pancakes in front of Sarah. "He tried to hide it but I've known him nearly all his life. I can read his moods pretty well. 'Course the fact that he's been sitting at this table staring at the same article for the past fifteen minutes and didn't eat but half of his pancakes were both pretty obvious signs."

Sarah frowned at the back door through which the taciturn cowhand had so recently exited. "Looks like this could be a real short date today." Seeing the regret in Ruth's eyes, she added, "I'm sorry our getting together isn't working out."

Ruth's expression became stern. "I meant it when I told you I didn't want you hooking up with Sam for Orville's and my sake." Ruth's expression relaxed and her voice took on a motherly tone. "I know you think I sound foolish but, like I said before, I've always thought you and Sam would make a good couple if you'd just learn to get along. But, I guess what ain't meant to be, just ain't meant to be."

"You can't make a silk purse out of a sow's ear," Sarah muttered, then grimaced self-consciously. "My grandmother would have been able to come up with a better adage."

"Eat before those pancakes get ice-cold," Ruth ordered. "I'm going to go see if Orville's finished shaving and is about ready for his breakfast."

As Ruth exited, Sarah stared at her food. Her appetite was gone, but she forced herself to take a bite. "I can't believe Ruth actually thought Sam and I would make a good couple," she mused aloud as she swallowed.

Something that felt a lot like disappointment began to pervade her. I'm just unhappy because I couldn't help Ruth and Orville, she assured herself. But she'd never been very good at lying to herself and she knew she wasn't being totally honest. "All right! All right! So I did think getting to know him could prove to be interesting and I'm a little down because I'm not going to get the chance," she admitted in a low grumble.

"On the other hand, I probably should be counting my blessings. Most likely he's a real bore and I probably would have regretted agreeing to help him," she reasoned as she swallowed a second bite. It felt like a rock in her stomach.

Anger toward Sam grew. If he wanted to call off his plan, why hadn't he just asked to see her in private and done it? He probably thought that because he asked her on a date, he had to go through with it out of politeness. Her jaw tensed. Well, she wasn't going to spend a day with a man who would rather be mucking out a barn than be with her.

Shoving her chair back, she rose, strode to the door, grabbed her coat from its peg and left. Assuming Sam was at his place, she crossed the space between the houses in long, purposeful strides.

When she reached his porch, Sam opened the door before she had a chance to knock. "You didn't have to come over here. I was going to come back to the main house and pick you up," he said with an irritated growl.

She glared up at him. "This arrangement isn't going to work. It's obvious you can barely tolerate my company. You're going to have to come up with another plan to get this ranch."

As she turned to walk away, his hand closed around her arm stopping her. "It's not your company I can't abide. It's being made to look like a fool."

Sarah stared at him in confusion. "I have no idea what you're talking about."

Forcefully he guided her into his house. Then kicking the door closed with the heel of his boot, he released her. "Last night it occurred to me that you might have agreed to go along with my courting you just to make Anders jealous."

"That's ridiculous." Sarah frowned at him. "I'm the one who walked out on him."

Sam didn't look convinced. "You've been pining over the man for better than twenty years."

"I wouldn't call it pining," she replied stiffly. "I just never found anyone I was attracted to strongly enough to marry. There was always this feeling that I had unfinished business here. So, I came back. I saw Ward for what he was, thanked my lucky stars I hadn't married him and put him out of my mind."

Sam studied her cynically. "You sure that down in that subconscious of yours, you don't want him crawling to you?"

Sarah glowered at him. "I don't play those kinds of games."

Sam's expression relaxed. "I'm glad to hear that. And now that we've cleared the air, are you ready to leave?"

Sarah's gaze narrowed on him. "That's it! No apology? No, I'm sorry, Sarah, for accusing you of trying to use me in an adolescent bid for attention?"

A sheepish grin played at one corner of his mouth. "I'm sorry, Sarah," he said gruffly.

He looked actually boyish, she thought in amazement. She'd never thought that was possible. "Apology accepted," she replied and marveled that the words had come out so calmly when her heart was racing so wildly.

"Now can we get started?" he prodded, nodding toward the door.

"I have to go back to the main house for my purse," she said, making a hurried exit.

Sam does seem to have a knack for making my adrenaline pump faster, she admitted as she made her way along the path between the two houses. The effect he had on her was decidedly disconcerting but, she had to confess, she hadn't felt this alive in a long time.

Orville and Ruth were in the kitchen when she entered. "I've just got to get my purse, then we're on our way," she informed them as she continued on through and up to her room.

Ruth met her at the foot of the steps when she came back down. "Did you find out what was bothering Sam?" her aunt asked, anxiously.

"It was just a male pride thing," Sarah replied, keeping her voice low to make certain Orville didn't overhear. "He was worried I was dating him to make Ward jealous and he didn't want to be made to look like a fool."

Ruth's expression suddenly became protective. "You aren't, are you?" she asked. "I know you told me you were finished with Ward, but maybe you were lying to yourself. I wouldn't want to see Sam get hurt."

"No, I wasn't lying to myself," Sarah assured her. "And neither of us is going to get hurt," she added. How could they? she reasoned. There was no emotional commitment involved. Not even a physical one. Her relationship with Sam was merely a business arrangement.

I just wish he didn't look so good, she thought as she and Ruth returned to the kitchen to find Sam there with Orville. "I'm ready," she announced and after a quick round of goodbyes, she and Sam were on their way out the back door.

He guided her to a blue pickup. It had a few years on it and when she climbed in, she noticed it had a lot of miles but it ran well as they pulled out onto the main road.

"Hope you don't mind making the trip in this old truck," he said, breaking the silence between them. "But I've got some supplies I need to pick up while we're in town."

The certainty that he was more interested in obtaining his supplies than spending time with her, irked her. "Knowing you have a truly important reason for making this trip takes the pressure off me. I'd hate to think you were wasting an entire day just to put on a good show for Orville," she returned dryly.

He glanced toward her with a questioning look as if he didn't understand what was bugging her.

What was wrong with her? She was acting as if she'd thought this was a real date. "I didn't mean that the way it came out. I guess I'm still a little nervous about our arrangement. I'm really glad you were able to find something useful to do today."

He accepted her explanation with a nod, then his expression became businesslike. "We never discussed how much I'd pay you for your time. Do you have a figure in mind?"

"I'm not sure what the going rate for make-believe wives is," she replied, uncertain of what to charge.

"What do you usually get paid?" he asked.

"A lot. But then I'm providing a medical service. In this instance, I'll simply be going about my life."

His jaw tensed. "I can afford to pay you two hundred a week for six months. I figure we can date for a couple of weeks then get married. Orville and Ruth have been looking at properties in Arizona every time they go to visit Ruth's sister. And Abigail keeps them apprised of anything that comes on the market that might interest them. I noticed Orville had information on a couple of small ranches. It's my guess he'll be quick to sell this place to me and get moved. This winter has been real hard on his arthritis."

Sarah nodded. "That seems reasonable."

"After he and Ruth have moved, you can go back to taking nursing assignments. Then a while after that we can apply for the divorce. Of course we'll need to keep that private for as long as possible." Sam continued. "If Orville finds out you're not still at the ranch, I'll tell him you loved your work too much to give it up entirely so you're taking jobs every once in a while. I can also say that the extra money helps us meet expenses. That way we can keep up the pretense of having a marriage to satisfy his conscience and keep Ruth happy."

"Sounds like you've got this worked out really well," Sarah said.

Sam suddenly frowned darkly. "I don't like fooling Orville. But that ranch is as much a part of me as an arm or a leg. And I know moving is what's best for him, too."

The guilt she heard in his voice touched her. "I'm sure Orville won't mind being tricked. He and Ruth both want you to have the place. It wasn't fair of my grandfather to place a restriction on him."

"Thanks." Sam grimaced crookedly. "I needed to hear that from a Perry."

Sarah experienced a curl of pleasure that she'd been able to ease his conscience. Then getting back to their original topic, she said, "A hundred a week should suffice. After all, you're just buying my time. I'll look at this assignment as a paid vacation. Lots of people shell out a small fortune to spend just a couple of weeks at a real ranch."

His jaw tensed with pride. "I'll pay you two hundred," he said firmly.

"Suit yourself," she replied, thinking she'd never met a more stubborn man.

As a silence again fell between them, she turned on the radio. For the next few minutes she tried to find a station that interested her. Mostly all she could get was static. Giving up, she switched the radio off and settled back in her seat.

She tried to concentrate on the road ahead but her attention kept shifting back to the man at the wheel. Covertly she studied his profile. An urge to run her finger along the hard, firm line of his jaw to test the texture of his skin shook her. She was allowed to look but not touch, she reminded herself. And she'd probably be smart to not even look, she added, unnerved by the strength of her curiosity regarding the physical aspects of the man.

Think about something else! she ordered herself. "If this scheme works and you do get the ranch, do you have any improvements you're planning to make?" she asked.

"I'd like to run a bigger herd of cattle. And I'd like to get into the horse breeding business, too," he replied succinctly, his attention never leaving the road.

When he said no more, she frowned. Clearly he was not interested in conversing. Her gaze again fell on his jaw and Sarah found herself wondering what kind of response she would get from him if she did stroke it. Probably one that would be sure to embarrass her, she thought. Whether he wanted to talk or not, she was determined to keep the conversation going. "What kind of horses would you breed? Quarter horses? Or something more exotic like Appaloosas? Or Arabians, maybe?''

This time he did glance toward her. Then returning his attention to the road, he asked, ''Are you really interested or are you simply trying to make conversation?''

''I'm really interested in making conversation,'' she replied honestly. ''And I figure talking about your plans for the ranch is a safe topic.''

For a moment he hesitated, then, with a shrug, he said, ''I haven't really decided yet what kind of horses I want to breed. There's always a market for good quarter horses. Then again, I've heard a lot of wealthy people are looking for Arabians.''

Sensing he was going to become silent again, Sarah asked about the differences in the various breeds. Sam's voice warmed as he began describing them and pointing out the pros and cons of each.

''You do know a lot about horses,'' she said as they drove into Rawlins a while later.

''I hope I didn't bore you,'' he apologized stiffly. ''But you were the one who wanted conversation.''

''I wasn't bored,'' she assured him honestly.

''Truth is, talking this out with you has helped me,'' he admitted.

Sarah again experienced a flush of pleasure. ''I like to think you're getting your money's worth for my time,'' she bantered.

''I am,'' he replied.

The businesslike quality in his voice cooled her pleasure. Surely you didn't expect him to join in a bit of light jesting, maybe even a little flirting, she chided herself.

"I thought we'd pick up the supplies first, then we'd have the rest of the day to do whatever we like," he continued in the same businesslike vein.

"Sounds like a good plan to me," she replied.

Several hours later, sitting in the darkened movie theater, Sarah leaned back in her chair and shoveled a handful of popcorn into her mouth. Judging by the laughter coming from the rest of the audience, the show was good but she couldn't relax enough to enjoy it.

Picking up the supplies at the feed and hardware store had gone well. While Sam had taken care of buying what was needed and getting it loaded, she'd crossed the street to a Western clothing store and bought a couple more pairs of jeans, three shirts and a new pair of riding boots. She'd reasoned that if she was going to be staying at the ranch for a while, she needed a few more work clothes.

When their business was finished, Sam had suggested getting some lunch. For that they'd gone to a small diner down the street from where they'd been shopping.

They'd just seated themselves and were looking over the menu when Sarah noticed a flicker of uneasiness on Sam's face, then his expression became even more stoic than usual. Glancing in the direction he'd been looking, she saw a waitress approaching. The woman, Sarah judged, was in her mid to late thirties, obviously of Indian lineage and pretty.

"Well, Sam Raven, it's been a long time," the waitress said, her gaze traveling over him speculatively as she came to a halt at their table.

"Afternoon, May. I didn't know you were working here," he replied. There was an apology in his voice that suggested that had he known, he would have avoided the place.

Obviously these two have a history, Sarah mused, and a twinge that felt like jealousy twisted inside of her. I am not jealous, she assured herself. She simply didn't want to be part of an embarrassing scene. There had been a time or two in her youth when Sam had managed to irritate her enough that she'd wanted to take a swing at him. She just hoped their waitress hadn't been biding her time to extract that same sort of revenge.

Suddenly the woman smiled. "Don't worry, Sam. There was a time when I'd gladly have taken this opportunity to slap you. But that was a lot of years ago. I've got a good husband and two great kids. And we're living here in Rawlins. I always wanted to live in town."

Sam visibly relaxed. "I'm glad you're happy."

Her smile suddenly took on a saucy quality. "I still think I was worth more than a couple of horses, though." Then with a light chuckle, she poised her pencil and asked what they wanted to eat.

As she left, Sarah studied Sam thoughtfully. When he remained silent, she ordered herself not to ask, but her curiosity was too strong. "Are you going to tell me what that was all about or leave it to my imagination?"

He shrugged as if to say what had happened between him and the woman named May was of little importance, then explained in an easy drawl, "When I was in my early twenties, my grandmother decided I needed a wife. Among her people there is an old tradition that grandparents choose the wives of their grandsons. However, the way this usually works is that the grandson finds a woman he wishes to marry then takes her to meet his grandparents and they say, 'Ah, yes, she is the one.'"

"In other words, they give their approval of their grandson's choice rather than actually searching out a bride," Sarah clarified.

Sam nodded and his drawl took on an impatient edge. "But my grandmother has always been a strong-willed woman. When she makes up her mind about something, she acts. So instead of waiting for me to choose someone, she chose for me. And she chose May. She talked to May's parents and they agreed. By the time I was told what was going on, the deal was cut. Out of respect for my grandmother, I agreed to consider the match and began to court May. But, although she's a real nice person, I couldn't see myself spending my life with her. We wanted to walk different paths. Like she just said, she wanted to live in town. I like the open spaces. So I called the whole thing off. Her family was furious. It cost me two good horses to make peace with them."

"You seem to be either buying your way out of marriage or into it," Sarah observed.

Sam acknowledged this remark with a dry look but made no response.

"Have you ever been in love?" Sarah gulped mentally. She couldn't believe she'd asked such a personal question of Sam. But what really shook her was how interested she was in his answer.

His gaze leveled on her and he studied her in a cool silence.

Obviously he thinks I'm being overly nosy, she fussed at herself. And I am, she admitted, angry at her attempt to invade his privacy.

Just when she was sure he wasn't going to answer, he said abruptly, "Not that I know of." Then he took out a pamphlet he'd picked up at the hardware store and began reading it, marking an end to any further conversation.

Shocked by how pleased his answer made her, Sarah shifted her gaze to the street beyond the window. But she barely noticed the people or cars as thoughts of Sam's grandmother began to nag her. Although Sarah knew of her, she'd never met White Flower. She knew Sam's mother had died in childbirth and his maternal grandparents had passed away several years before that. She was also aware that being a member of the Tribal Police Force as well as a practicing shaman had required his father to be away from home a great deal. Thus, Sam had been raised mostly by his paternal grandmother. "How will White Flower feel about you marrying me?" A second thought occurred to her and she added, "Or will you tell her the truth about our marriage?"

Sam looked up from the pamphlet. "We've promised Ruth that Orville will not find out, so I will not tell my grandmother. There is a chance she would tell my father or a close friend and the truth would spread."

Sarah nodded. "A secret shared is no longer a secret."

Unexpectedly Sam grinned. "A man who speaks his thoughts aloud cannot control how far his words will travel."

Behind his smile Sarah saw the challenge in his eyes. The man was full of surprises, she thought as she realized he was playing the adage game. The problem was she found herself so fascinated by the deep brown color of his eyes, she couldn't think. In a moment you're going to start to drool, she warned herself.

To her relief, May returned with their coffee. As the woman left, her original worry returned. "You didn't answer my question about how your grandmother will react to our marriage," she said stiffly.

The amusement left his face. "She'll accept my decision," he replied.

Sarah heard the hard edge in his voice. "But she won't like the fact that you're not marrying within the Indian nation."

His gaze leveled on her. "Sarah, I'm a grown man. Although I prefer not to antagonize my grandmother, I will choose my own path."

Her gaze traveled along the strong line of his jaw. The strength of purpose she saw there left no doubt in her mind that he would allow no one to deter him from any route he chose.

Now, seated in the darkened movie theater, shoving popcorn into her mouth, she again found her attention drawn to his profile. He didn't look any more relaxed than she was. A burst of laughter issued from the other patrons but he didn't even smile.

Her own tension grew. What had she gotten herself into? Six months of stress and strain, came the answer. How in the world could I have thought this would be an adventure? she mocked herself.

Unexpectedly he leaned toward her. "You don't seem to be enjoying this movie any more than I am," he whispered in her ear. "And there's a chance of new snow. Maybe we should start home."

His words took a moment to register. When he'd spoken, his warm breath against her skin had sent an unexpected current of delight coursing through her. Barely managing not to choke on the popcorn she'd been eating, she nodded her consent. As she followed him out of the theater, she could still feel a tingling sensation along the sensitive cord of her neck.

Other men had whispered in her ear but she'd never experienced such a strong reaction, she admitted as they walked back to his truck. There was no use trying to deny it any longer—she felt a physical attraction toward the man.

An incredibly strong one, she confessed as he opened the door of the truck then placed a hand on her arm to give her a lift up. Even through the fabric of her sweater and coat, she was acutely aware of his touch. Well, she was a normal, healthy female, she reminded herself. Being attracted to a virile male was natural.

An idea that would make their marriage a real adventure began to germinate. All the way home and into the night it tormented her. One minute she'd tell her-

self she'd found a perfect solution to a problem that
had been bothering her lately. The next moment, she'd
become wary and argue that Sam Raven was not a
good solution.

## *Chapter Six*

Sarah drew a shaky breath as she took one last look at herself in her bedroom mirror. She was more nervous today than she'd ever been before one of her visits to Miss Jocelyn.

For the three days following their trip into town, Sam had invited her over to his place in the evenings. There they'd watched movies on video, played gin rummy, or she'd watched television while he sat by the fire and worked on one of his carvings. They hadn't talked much. She knew he was simply biding his time until he felt they could announce their engagement. As for herself, although she experienced an underlying tension, she was surprised by how much she liked being in his home.

Then last night he'd informed her that today they would be going to visit White Flower. "I have to go see my grandmother. My father watches over her, but his duties as a shaman take him away from home a great deal. I go to visit her once every couple of weeks to check on her and take her supplies," he'd explained.

Sarah saw a flicker of uneasiness cross his features, then his expression became unreadable again. "You'll have to come with me. She would expect me to bring any woman I was considering for a bride to meet her. And you going with me should convince Orville that I have serious feelings toward you," he'd finished.

Sarah had always been curious about Sam's family. Excitement had swirled through her. She was actually going to meet his grandmother. Then she'd recalled the momentary flash of uneasiness on his face and her excitement had dampened. Despite his assurance at the diner, clearly he was worried about this meeting. She guessed he was only going through with it because he felt it was necessary to convince Orville.

And he'd been right about Orville's reaction. When she'd returned to the main house, Orville had been sitting by the wood-burning stove in the kitchen whittling. He'd waved her into the other rocking chair. "You and Sam seem to be getting along real fine," he'd said as she seated herself.

"We are," she'd assured him.

He'd stopped whittling then to look her in the eye. "I have to admit, I'm a mite surprised by this turn of events. But I can't say I'm sorry. The two of you make a fine-looking pair."

She'd seen the hopeful gleam in his eyes. "He has to take some supplies to his grandmother tomorrow," she'd said. "And I'm going along."

The gleam in Orville's eyes had brightened. "So you two are serious."

"It looks that way." Then because her meeting with Sam's grandmother was so strong on her mind, she'd heard herself adding honestly, "But I am a little nervous about meeting his family."

Orville had grinned. "Now don't you fret. I'll admit White Flower can be a bit intimidating." Returning to his whittling, he'd chuckled. "She looks older than the hills but she's still full of salt. When she speaks, everyone within earshot jumps to her orders." His gaze returned to Sarah. "But you'll do just fine. You've got the Perry grit."

Sarah had silently moaned. In her own way, it would seem that White Flower was very much like Miss Jocelyn. Now she fully understood Sam's uneasiness. He expected trouble. "I appreciate your confidence," she'd said, easing herself out of the chair. Then giving him a hug, she'd bid him goodnight and gone upstairs.

She'd slept restlessly and woken early. On an impulse she'd gone down to the kitchen and made corn bread muffins to take to White Flower. She'd meant to keep them plain but her nerves had gotten the better of her and she'd thrown in some parsley and basil at the last minute.

"Why couldn't White Flower have been the sweet little grandmotherly type?" she groaned as she took one final glance in the mirror. Her makeup was lightly applied and her lipstick was a muted shade somewhere between red and pink. She'd chosen slacks over jeans. Casual but not too casual was how she'd wanted to appear and she felt she'd succeeded. With the slacks, she was wearing a simple unadorned sweater and a pair of Western-cut boots. Finally, she'd pulled her hair loosely back and tied it with a ribbon at her nape, letting it hang down the center of her back.

"Sam's here," Ruth yelled from the foot of the steps.

"I'll be right down," she called back. Taking another calming breath, she abruptly frowned at herself. This meeting wasn't that important. After all, her marriage to Sam was merely a ploy to soothe Orville's conscience.

She should look at this expedition as merely a part of the adventure, she told herself. And in spite of her anxiousness about facing White Flower, she had to admit she actually wanted to go. In fact, she'd be disappointed if she weren't going. She'd always wondered what Sam's life away from the ranch had been like. The truth was, when she'd been young, living here with her grandparents, she wondered about it a great deal.

Even during the years she'd been away, he'd popped into her mind occasionally...usually when she'd done something stupid and gotten herself in trouble. In her mind's eyes, she'd seen him standing there with that "I knew this was going to happen" expression on his face. Several years ago, during one of these moments, it had occurred to her that he might have learned that look from seeing it on his grandmother's face when he'd been a boy.

And now she would be able to test that theory first-hand. This was definitely an opportunity she would not have wanted to pass up. "Of course, curiosity did kill the cat," she muttered, then scowled at herself. She'd faced Miss Jocelyn and survived. Besides, it didn't matter if Sam's grandmother approved or disapproved of her. She was merely playing a part in a charade.

Her nervousness again under control, the twinkle of excitement returned to her eyes. Grabbing her purse, she went downstairs.

But a little later, as she and Sam drove toward the reservation, her nervousness began to build once again. She'd grown used to Sam's reticence. In fact, she'd brought a book along to read when she got tired of watching the scenery. But she couldn't concentrate on the words. Covertly she glanced at him.

His jaw was set in a purposeful line reminding her of a soldier preparing himself for battle. The sudden realization that his tension was what was causing her nervousness, shook her. When had she become so attuned to his moods? she wondered.

He'd always affected her strongly. In the past, though, the effect had been to irritate. Now she found herself sensing his worry and wishing she could help.

"My grandmother can be cantankerous," he said, abruptly breaking his silence.

"So I've heard," she replied levelly.

He glanced over at her. "Are you feeling all right?"

Surprised by the question, she studied him narrowly. "I'm fine."

"You've never passed up an opportunity like that before." Again he glanced at her as if worried she was ill. "I figured you'd at least make some crack about cantankerousness obviously being a family trait."

He was right, she realized. But today, instead of taking a jab at him, she wanted to be his friend. "I guess I figured it was time I started practicing restraint. We are in this together."

"Yeah," he said, his jaw hardening even more.

He looked like a man who saw himself as walking toward the gates of hell, she thought. "You must be expecting your grandmother to be violently opposed to this marriage. Perhaps you should reconsider telling her the truth," she suggested.

He continued to stare at the road ahead. "It's not my grandmother I'm concerned about," he said gruffly. "You're a good woman, Sarah Orman. I feel guilty putting you through this ordeal."

Her eyes rounded in surprise. "You paid me a compliment with no catch attached."

A sheepish grin tilted one corner of his mouth. Then his expression became serious once again. "I had hoped my father would be present. My grandmother is sometimes more diplomatic when he's around. But he's away."

Sarah told herself that his family was none of her business, still she heard herself asking, "Do you have any other family living on the reservation or nearby?"

"No. Since my grandfather passed away, my father and my grandmother are my only close relatives still remaining here. There are some distant cousins but I rarely see them. Most have left." His jaw suddenly relaxed as if he'd found a solution to their dilemma. "There is a café on the way to my grandmother's place. I could drop you off there and pick you up on the way home."

Sarah had to admit that she was more nervous than ever about facing Sam's grandmother, but her curiosity was stronger than ever. "I have no intention of sitting around a diner all day," she said firmly. "Besides, Orville and Ruth are both bound to ask questions about how the meeting went and I don't feel like making up a whole passel of lies."

Sam's jaw tensed once again and he nodded grimly. "You're right. Besides, there's always the chance she'll decide to come to the wedding. That would not be the place for a first meeting."

"Definitely not the place," Sarah agreed.

Again a silence descended between them. Sarah returned her attention to her book but the words refused to register. Instead Sam's voice saying she was a good woman kept replaying through her mind. She told herself she was being silly but the compliment brought her a great deal of pleasure. Giving up her attempt to read, she stared out the window at the cold landscape.

She had known the drive to the reservation would be long, but it had seemed interminable, she thought when they finally pulled up in front of a small, single story, frame house.

Insisting on helping, she carried one of the boxes of supplies while Sam carried two others. Before they were halfway to the porch, the door opened. A frail Indian woman, stooped with age, who looked as if she could be carried away by a light breeze, was framed in the doorway.

"Hurry yourselves up," she called out to them, waving her cane in a gesture meant to speed them along. "I don't want to be letting all my heat out."

As Sam and Sarah entered, the old woman stepped back. When they were inside, she shoved the door closed with her cane.

Sarah felt a prickling on the back of her neck as she set the box she was carrying on the table. Turning, she found White Flower carefully scrutinizing her. To take in all of Sarah's five feet nine inches, the elderly woman had to retreat a step.

Sam set his boxes down quickly and took a position beside Sarah. "Grandmother, this is Sarah Orman. Sarah, this is my grandmother, Mary White Flower Raven," he said, introducing the two women.

Interest sparked in the deep brown eyes that continued to study Sarah. "Sarah Orman," White Flower repeated.

Sam placed an arm around Sarah's waist. "I am going to marry Sarah," he said with a finality that let his grandmother know he did not want any argument.

Sarah stood mutely. She ordered herself to speak but her mind refused to function. All she could think of was the strong, hard feel of Sam's arm draped around her back and the firmness in his voice. She could not remember feeling so protected. It's the ranch he's really thinking about, she reminded herself curtly. She forced a smile and said politely, "I'm looking forward to becoming a member of your family."

"Sarah Orman . . . yes, of course," White Flower murmured, speaking more to herself than to the others. She waved her cane at a chair and couch grouping. "Sit," she ordered, then hobbled to a rocking chair near the fireplace.

"Sarah baked you some corn bread muffins," Sam said as Sarah seated herself on the couch and he started to join her.

"Bring me one," White Flower ordered.

Straightening, Sam went to the boxes of supplies, took out a muffin and carried it to his grandmother.

Sarah was aware of the elderly woman constantly watching her and her nerves grew taut. "I hope you enjoy them," she said levelly.

White Flower looked at the muffin, then sniffed it. "Herbs. You put herbs in it."

Mentally Sarah kicked herself. She'd told herself to leave them plain but she hadn't listened!

"I like herbs in my food," White Flower announced abruptly.

Sarah had seen Sam tense as if ready to do battle; now he was once again merely on guard. So far, so good, she told herself encouragingly.

Continuing to hold the muffin without eating it, White Flower's gaze again returned to Sarah. "So you are Sarah Orman," she repeated once again. "I have wondered about you."

Out of the corner of her eye, Sarah noticed Sam shift as if he was uncomfortable. "You know who I am?" she asked, wondering if at least some of Sam's uneasiness was because, through the years, he'd been telling his grandmother of their skirmishes. Or maybe he'd simply told White Flower that he considered her a pest.

"I am not a healer as my husband was and my son is, but I have spoken with the spirits," White Flower said. "And there are those who come to me for help or advice. Four times, Sam has asked me to create a spell that would protect you."

Shocked by this revelation, Sarah turned to Sam.

"You were always doing something I figured was going to get your neck broken," he elaborated stiffly. "The roundups were particularly scary."

Sarah was still assimilating this information when White Flower, again speaking more to herself than to the others, said as if recalling more information stored deeply, "You were in the military." She chuckled lightly. "I remember one of his requests came when he learned you'd been stationed where terrorist activity was high. He said if a bomb was going to be planted within fifty miles of you, you'd probably manage to be on ground zero."

Sam scowled at his grandmother and Sarah, to her amazement, saw a flush of embarrassment spreading from his neck upward. "I never pictured you as the guardian angel type," she said, regarding him thoughtfully. In spite of the strong streak of independence that ran through her, the knowledge that in his own way he'd been looking after her, caused a warm glow to spread through her.

Sam shrugged a shoulder. "Your grandfather ordered all of us who worked for him to keep an eye on you especially during roundups. I just got used to feeling responsible. Besides, you were an orphan. Among my people that makes you the responsibility of all."

The warm glow vanished. Obviously he had not enjoyed the responsibility he'd felt thrust on him. And she most certainly did not need him or anyone watching over her, she told herself.

"Rumbling Thunder has always taken his responsibilities very seriously," White Flower spoke up. "However, he has not always accepted my guidance," she added with a reproving frown.

Sure the old woman was talking about the marriage she'd attempted to arrange for her grandson, Sarah braced herself for an onslaught of disapproval. Out of the corner of her eye, she noticed Sam's shoulders straighten and knew he was preparing himself to meet his grandmother's objections to his chosen wife.

White Flower breathed a resigned sigh and, although her frown remained, it did soften. "But he is a man now and he knows his own mind and heart."

Sarah breathed a mental sigh of relief as Sam relaxed. Clearly White Flower did not truly approve of the match but she was willing to accept it. Sarah's stomach grumbled, reminding her of the time. Grateful for an excuse to move around, she rose and headed toward the boxes of supplies. "Ruth sent some food for lunch. I'll heat it."

White Flower merely nodded and began nibbling on the corn bread muffin.

"You're a nurse," the old woman said unexpectedly as Sarah poured Ruth's homemade chicken soup into a pan. "That is in keeping with our family tradition. Of course, you practice white man's medicine.

But, in all fairness, I will admit there are times when your potions work quite well.''

Sarah looked back at White Flower. The woman was staring into the fire.

As if she sensed Sarah's gaze, White Flower turned to her. "And you look healthy," she added.

"Thanks" was all Sarah could think to reply. Quickly she returned her attention to preparing the food.

Sam began asking his grandmother about others in the community and Sarah was relieved to have the focus of attention removed from her. She had actually begun to relax by the time she announced lunch was ready.

As the three sat at the table, White Flower took a few sips of her soup, smiled with satisfaction, then leveled her gaze on Sarah once again. "You look as if you still have some childbearing years left. I've always wanted great-grandchildren."

Feeling as if she'd been issued an ultimatum, Sarah forced a noncommittal smile.

White Flower nodded sharply to give emphasis to her words then returned to concentrating on her food.

Sam gave Sarah an "I'm sorry about that" glance, then he, too, returned to eating.

Swallowing a spoonful of soup, Sarah unexpectedly found herself imagining holding a dark-haired, brown-eyed baby in her arms while a feeling of motherly love threatened to overwhelm her. That would be going too far, she admonished herself, and shoved the image from her mind.

But later as she and Sam drove home, that image came back. It was followed by seeing Sam holding the hand of a dark-haired toddler as the two walked toward a corral filled with horses. A warm, loving feeling spread through her.

I'm obviously having a midlife crisis, she wailed silently, and shoved the images out of her mind.

# Chapter Seven

Sarah stood staring at herself in her bedroom mirror. She was too numb to be nervous. Today was her wedding day.

A week after she and Sam had visited White Flower they'd announced their engagement. "We've decided to get married as quickly as possible," Sam had told Orville and Ruth. "We're not getting any younger and we don't see any sense in waiting."

"Can't say as I'm surprised," Orville had replied, shaking Sam's hand.

Ruth had smiled warmly and given them both a hug, but Sarah had seen the concern behind her happy facade.

Once the congratulations had been issued, a fatherly expression had come over Orville's face. "This courtship has been a mite fast and if you were different people I might caution you to wait a bit longer. But you've both always held your own counsel and I trust your judgment," he said.

"We're going to take care of getting our blood tests tomorrow, then get the license and make arrangements with the Justice of the County Court to marry us as soon as possible," Sam had explained.

"And we'd like for the two of you to stand with us and be our witnesses," Sarah had finished.

Ruth's jaw had suddenly firmed. "You'll have the wedding here. We'll get some flowers in. I'll fix a nice meal and we'll have a cake."

"And if it's all right with you two, we'll get Reverend Phillips to officiate," Orville suggested. "He's been baptizing, marrying and burying folks around here for better than thirty years."

Sarah had found herself feeling a little hypocritical about saying her vows in front of a man of God. "We really don't want to put you to any trouble," she'd protested.

"It's no trouble," Ruth insisted.

"You might as well let her have her way." Orville gave his wife's shoulders a squeeze. "Through the years, I've learned that's the easiest road to take."

Sarah had read the determination on Ruth's face. Besides, this could be her only wedding, she'd admitted to herself. It might as well feel like the real thing. "Having the wedding here would be lovely," she'd said and had given Ruth another hug.

The next day they'd begun making arrangements. Now, only a day later than she and Sam had originally planned, they were going to be married. The living room of the ranch was decorated with flowers. A roast was cooking in the oven, sending its fragrant aroma throughout the house. Henrietta Bluetail had been hired for the day to help with preparing the meal and serving it. And a two-tiered wedding cake, which Sarah and Ruth had created together, was sitting on the sideboard.

Sarah's gaze again traveled over her image in the mirror. She looked like a bride, she thought. She'd chosen a white linen suit with white heels. Her hair was swept up into a French twist and Ruth had insisted she wear the bridal veil Ruth had worn when she and Orville were wed. It was a double affair, covering her head all around and hanging to a few inches below her shoulders. A small circlet of pearls formed a crown that held it in place.

As many times as Sarah had reminded herself that this wedding was not to be taken too seriously, she still found herself wanting to follow the traditions. Besides, Ruth would have insisted on them anyway, she reasoned. So the veil was the something old and the something borrowed. The white silk blouse she was wearing with the suit was the something new. And she'd tied a small blue ribbon around her leg where she would have worn a garter.

Her gaze traveled from her reflection to her bed mirrored behind her. Lying there were the two roses, one white and one red, tied together with white and silver ribbon, she would be carrying as her bouquet. Turning away from the mirror, she walked to the bed, picked them up and breathed in their fragrant aroma. Their arrival this morning had come with a surprise.

Sam had left the arrangements for the flowers up to Ruth and Sarah and she'd been certain he hadn't given her bridal bouquet a thought.

But when the delivery from the florist had arrived, her bouquet had been boxed separately from the men's boutonnieres and the pink rose Ruth was to carry. And when Sarah had taken her roses out of the box, she'd discovered a note inside. It was handwritten from Sam. *Thank you,* it said.

His image suddenly filled her mind and a fresh wave of nervousness assailed her. We're not entering into a lifetime commitment, she reminded herself. This is merely a small adventure. His image became sharper. Well, maybe not a *small* adventure, she corrected with a crooked smile.

A knock on the door cut into her thoughts. Glad to have a diversion, she called out, "Come in."

Ruth entered. An apron protected the front of the blue wool dress she'd chosen to wear for the ceremony and Sarah guessed her aunt had recently been in the kitchen checking on the dinner. Confirming this suspicion, Ruth said, "The food is coming along nicely. Henrietta has everything under control."

Sarah saw the shadow of uneasiness cross Ruth's face. "Is something wrong?"

"I don't think so," Ruth replied. Her nervousness now clearly visible, she said, "I don't know. Sam's father, John Raven, and White Flower have arrived."

Sarah's stomach knotted as a vision of the wedding turning into a brawl filled her mind. Wondering if Ruth was having the same thought, she hid her own concern behind a mask of dry humor and asked, "Are you worried that when we reach the part of the ceremony where the minister says if there is anyone here who objects to this marriage they should rise now and speak, that either or both of them will bolt out of their seats?"

"The thought has occurred to me," Ruth replied. The concern in her eyes deepened and she took Sarah's hands in hers. "I know it's a little late for me to be asking this, but I have to know the truth. Are you really certain you know what you're doing?"

"No. But I do want to do it," Sarah replied honestly.

Ruth's jaw hardened. "I don't want you doing this just for Orville and me."

Sarah met her aunt's eyes levelly. "I'm not. I'm marrying Sam because I want to."

Ruth's gaze bore into her niece. "You aren't lying to me just to make me feel better, are you?" she demanded.

A self-conscious flush reddened Sarah's cheeks. "I almost wish I was," she admitted, then heard herself adding, "A part of me thinks I'm crazy but I really do want to marry Sam."

Ruth's jaw relaxed. "Then I wish you every joy," she said as she gave Sarah another hug. Releasing her niece, she glanced at her watch. "Orville said he would be waiting for us at the foot of the stairs at 2:25 exactly." She drew a calming breath and tossed her apron on the bed. "It's time to go."

"Well, don't you two look as pretty as a picture," Orville greeted them with an approving grin when they descended the stairs.

Sarah's smile suddenly felt plastic. In a few minutes she'd actually be married to Sam Raven.

"Never thought I'd see this day...Sam and Sarah getting hitched," Orville said with a chuckle.

My thoughts exactly, Sarah admitted silently. Craning her neck, she peeked through the entrance into the living room. Her blood began to race. Sam was wearing his Sunday suit and she didn't think she'd ever seen a man look more handsome. Or more virile, she added.

"There's been a slight change in the arrangements," Orville said, breaking into her thoughts.

Her attention immediately swung to her uncle. "Is there a problem?" she asked, wondering if White Flower and John Raven had already begun to voice their objections.

Orville smiled reassuringly. "Not a problem. It's just that John Raven requested that he stand by his son during the ceremony. He wants you to know that you are welcomed into his family." His smile warmed. "As for me, I get the honor of giving you away, then I get to sit down."

Sarah saw the faint grimace of pain cross his face as he shifted his weight and she knew his arthritis was causing him discomfort. I am definitely doing the right thing by marrying Sam, she reaffirmed, and her tension eased a little. "Thank you for making this day so nice for me," she said, giving her uncle a hug.

Looking a great deal more relaxed than she had been a few minutes earlier, Ruth took a final moment to make certain Sarah's veil was properly in place. Stepping back, she nodded her approval. "And now we're ready," she announced.

Staying a little behind, Sarah and Orville took a position behind Ruth as she moved to the doorway of the living room.

Beyond her aunt, Sarah could see Sam and the man standing beside him. John Raven was an older version of his son—tall, strongly built with a thick head of hair now fully gray. His Indian name, she knew, was Bear Stalker, and it seemed to suit him. He was dressed in a suit but wore a beaded necklace in place of a tie. He stood ramrod straight and there was a distinguished air about him. All in all, he was a little intimidating.

Glancing to an upholstered chair positioned a little away from the trio of men standing in the center of the room, she saw White Flower. As the men noticed Ruth and took their positions in preparation of Sarah's arrival, the elderly woman stood and walked toward the hall.

Sarah stiffened. Had White Flower come to stop the wedding or merely put a curse on her? she wondered. She realized Sam must have had the same thought. A dark scowl came over his features and he started toward his grandmother. But before he could take a second stride, his father placed a restraining hand on his arm and whispered something in Sam's ear.

Sarah saw Sam freeze but he did not relax. Instead he watched with a guarded expression, reminding her of a man braced for action.

Her gaze shifting to her aunt, Sarah saw Ruth's shoulders straighten as she stood firmly in the doorway, blocking White Flower's path. An increased pressure on her arm let her know that Orville stood ready to champion her also.

"I wish to speak to my future granddaughter," White Flower requested, forced to come to a halt in front of Ruth.

Ruth's shoulders squared even more while Orville's hold became firmer.

Their show of protection was heartwarming, Sarah thought, but no one could put off the inevitable. And the look of determination on White Flower's face made it clear that whatever she had to say, she was going to say. Sarah gave her uncle a reassuring smile, freed herself from his hold and stepped forward. Placing a hand on Ruth's arm, she gently urged her aunt to move to one side. She felt Ruth's muscles tighten momentarily in reluctance, then, with a protective gleam in her eyes, Ruth shifted to allow the elderly woman to pass.

"You have your traditions and I have mine," White Flower said. Reaching into the pouch she was carrying, she took out a beaded necklace with several large teeth strung into the design. "The bear has always been a strong totem among my ancestors," she said. "This necklace was worn by my mother and her mother before at their weddings. I wore it and Sam's mother wore it. Now I pass it on to you. May it bring a blessing to your mating."

Both Ruth and Orville visibly relaxed.

Leaning forward and lifting her veil so that White Flower could fasten the necklace around her neck, Sarah experienced a rush of guilt. "I am honored," she said sincerely, making a mental note to return the necklace to Sam so that it would remain in his family.

White Flower nodded with satisfaction then returned to her chair.

Sarah saw Sam again take his position by the reverend. Stepping back, she allowed Ruth to again take the lead. As soon as White Flower was seated comfortably, Ruth walked with sedate dignity to the men, then turned to watch as Sarah and Orville joined the group.

Sarah's nerves grew more tense as the ceremony began. Telling herself she was merely edgy because they'd had no time for a rehearsal, she concentrated on what the reverend was saying.

Finishing his small but pointed sermon about the sanctity of marriage, the reverend paused and smiled. "Sam. Sarah. Please join hands," he instructed.

Sarah handed her flowers to her aunt, then allowed Sam to take her hands in his. As they touched, a heat so intense her legs threatened to weaken, spread through her. She had never been the fainting type and she wasn't about to start now, she admonished herself, stunned by the intensity of her reaction. And, it wasn't Sam, so much as the fact that they were actually being wed that had her so thoroughly shaken, she added.

The reverend began guiding them through their vows and, as she knew was required of her at this point, she looked up into Sam's face. His expression was polite, with a touch of stiffness anyone who knew him would have expected on this occasion. Then he winked at her.

She knew it was meant merely as a comradely gesture but her heart did a lurch. Without even thinking, she winked back. His stiffness slackened and she realized he'd been worried she might bolt from the room at the last moment.

That he considered her so flighty she would change her mind at the last moment and not carry through on their agreement, irked her. The weakness in her legs vanished and a coolness descended over her. She cast him a dry look, then again concentrated on what the reverend was saying.

Following the minister's lead, Sam recited his vows then slipped the ring on her finger.

Sarah had expected to feel nothing but, as she watched and felt the gold band being placed on her finger, the wedding suddenly seemed very real to her. Until this moment, she'd been able to think of it as merely a scene in a play. Unable to shake the feeling of reality, a nervous edge entered her voice as she said her vows. When she slipped the ring on Sam's finger, her hand trembled slightly.

"And now I pronounce you husband and wife," the reverend intoned with a smile.

Again the sensation of embarking on an adventure swept through Sarah. She looked up at Sam. An uneasiness flicked in his eyes, then his expression became shuttered. Obviously he'd just had a bout of reality as well and realized that they were legally married, she decided. And he's suddenly not so sure this was a good idea, she added. Well, he was the one who'd worked out this strategy. She was just along as hired help. And I should keep that in mind at all times, she ordered herself as her sense of adventure again faded. "You may kiss the bride," the reverend instructed.

Sarah stiffened. Earlier she'd been looking forward to this moment. How his kiss affected her was the factor on which she'd been going to base her future actions. Now she merely wanted to get it over with.

And he clearly feels the same, she thought, seeing the uneasiness again flicker in his eyes. It'll probably feel like I'm being kissed by cardboard anyway, she told herself.

Wrong! her inner voice admitted as his mouth met hers. His lips were warm and inviting. A hunger for more swept through her and she had to fight the urge to move fully into his arms.

To her relief, he kept the kiss short. Not a peck but not a lover's kiss, either. One could classify it as polite. Still, the imprint of his lips lingered on hers and even after he'd completely released her, a slow curl of heat continued to work its way to the tips of her toes.

The strength of her physical attraction for him shook her. But she had her pride. This marriage would go the way he'd planned—she'd make no attempt to change the rules.

Forcing a smile, she again assumed the role of the happy bride.

* * *

"I'm glad that's over," Sarah muttered under her breath. Above her, stars filled the night sky. Ruth's dinner had gone very well. Fairly soon after the cake cutting, White Flower and Sam's father had again wished Sam and Sarah well, then left. Sam and Sarah had announced their intent to leave soon after that.

Now they were on their way to Sam's place. He was carrying a picnic basket heavily loaded with leftovers as well as a bottle of champagne Orville had added. She was carrying the top tier of the wedding cake, all wrapped and ready to be frozen so that it could be eaten on their first anniversary.

"Almost over," Sam corrected.

She glanced up at him questioningly.

They'd reached his porch and he nodded toward the door. "The threshold. If I know Ruth, she's just enough of a romantic to want to watch me carry you over it."

Sarah knew he was right but she wasn't looking forward to having him touch her. Attempting to maintain the appearance of a happily newlywed couple, they'd been forced to be in close proximity for the past several hours. Each time his hand had brushed hers or their shoulders had touched, she'd experienced what felt like currents of heated electricity shooting through her. Anger at herself for having such a strong attraction to a man who saw her merely as a necessary nuisance, boiled within her. Still, she could not entirely control her body's response to him.

Sam set the basket down on the porch and opened the door. Returning to where she was steeling herself to ignore him, he scooped her up in his arms and carried her inside.

The strength of his arms brought a fresh rush of sensual delight. Stop that! she ordered her body, but as he set her on the floor and returned to the porch for the basket, she noticed her legs threatened to wobble. Scowling at herself, she carried the cake into the kitchen and shoved it into the freezer.

Following her, he set the basket on the table. "And now we can relax," he said with relief.

His calmness grated on her taut nerves. She knew she wasn't being fair. She should also be feeling relieved to have made it through the wedding without incident. She took a deep breath to quail the muddle of emotions swirling within her. But as the afternoon began to replay through her mind, she recalled the wink, and the ire it had caused came back sharply. She told herself to forget it, but instead she turned to him accusingly. "You thought I was going to bolt, didn't you?"

"I couldn't be certain your wanderlust wouldn't suddenly become too strong for you to commit yourself to staying here even for just a few months," he replied honestly.

His lack of trust in her word hurt. She glared at him. "I'm not a flighty person. Once I make a commitment, I stick to it." Another memory returned and she faced him dryly. "Or maybe you were hoping that I would bolt. I could have sworn that as we said our final vows you were suddenly wondering if getting this ranch was worth marrying me."

He shifted uncomfortably. "You've always made me a little uneasy."

He'd confirmed all of her suspicions! "This is going to be one terrific marriage," she muttered sarcastically. Tossing him a final haughty glance as she headed for the door, she added over her shoulder, "I'm going to shower then curl up with a good book."

# *Chapter Eight*

Sarah tossed and turned restlessly. Finally giving in to her inability to sleep, she sat up in bed and switched on the light. Luckily the guest bedroom was toward the back side of the house. She was sure Ruth and Orville would not be able to see that it was in use.

Quietly she groaned. How could she have possibly thought being married to Sam Raven would be an adventure? Seeking a diversion to help her relax, she glanced at the book on the bedside table. She hadn't been able to concentrate on it earlier and it held no appeal for her now. Her stomach growled, reminding her she'd eaten very little at the dinner following the wedding.

She frowned at the door. "I've been hiding out in here," she admitted to herself. "Well, I can't stay in here forever," she added admonishingly.

Besides, Sam had retired for the night. He'd knocked on her door over an hour ago to ask if she needed anything. When she'd said she was fine, he'd informed her that he was going to bed and would leave the bathroom light on so that she could find her way down the hall.

Tossing off the covers, she rose. The urge to dress was strong. Again she scowled at herself. This house was going to be her home for the next few months. She'd better learn to be comfortable here. Taking her heavy terry-cloth robe from the closet, she pulled it on over the cotton nightgown she was wearing. Then after slipping her feet into her favorite snug, fluffy slippers, she opened the door.

Silence greeted her. Even though she was sure Sam was asleep, she paused to look across the hall to the door of the master bedroom. It was closed and there was no light coming from underneath it. Satisfied that she had the rest of the house to herself, she quietly made her way to the kitchen. There she discovered that Sam had unpacked the picnic basket and put the food away.

Well, at least he's not a slob, she thought. He was, however, boorish, she decided.

Pushing him to the back of her mind, she put some water on for tea. While waiting for it to boil, she made herself a sandwich. She'd just taken her first bite when the door opened and Sam strode in.

Grudgingly she wished he *looked* boorish. Obviously he'd dressed hastily. His feet were bare, his shirt was unbuttoned and the shirttail was hanging out over his jeans. That combined with his rumpled hair caused him to look unexpectedly appealing.

But he doesn't find me appealing, she reminded herself, and jerked her attention back to her sandwich.

"Are you finding everything you need?" he asked.

There was a gruffness in his voice and she guessed he didn't like being woken. Her shoulders straightened with pride. "Yes, thank you. There was really no need for you to get out of bed."

Out of the corner of her eye she saw his gaze travel around the kitchen. It stopped at the stove.

"If you're heating water for tea, I don't have any," he said.

"When I moved my things in yesterday, I checked your supplies," she replied. "And I brought some tea bags over from the main house."

"Good." He backed toward the door. "Since you seem to be making yourself at home, I'll just go back to bed."

He muttered a quick good-night and she tossed one back at him, then he was gone.

The water began to boil and she made herself a cup of tea. Then sitting at the table, she ate her sandwich and sipped on the hot brew. As she finished her sandwich, her gaze shifted to the large chunk of wedding cake Henrietta had packed in the picnic basket. Her tenseness had activated her sweet tooth. The temptation to eat the whole thing was strong. Controlling the impulse, she got out a plate and cut herself a medium-size piece.

Again seating herself at the table, she wished they'd put a double layer of icing on the cake. "And a few chocolate fudge flowers would have been nice, too," she muttered.

Abruptly the door opened again and Sam strode back into the room. "Are you sure you're all right?" he demanded impatiently. "It's nearly midnight. You should be asleep."

She rewarded his impatience with a haughty glance. "I'm just feeling a little restless. I'm sorry if I disturbed you, but there's no reason for you to concern yourself."

His jaw hardened. "This marriage is going to be a lot harder than I thought," he grumbled.

Ire sparked in her eyes. "Why don't you just go back to bed and forget I'm even here."

"I wish I could," he growled.

"I'm not the one in this room who is difficult to get along with," she snapped back.

His expression darkened further. "I didn't say you were."

Sarah scowled. She started to argue this point when the words suddenly caught in her throat. There was a heat in his eyes that matched the fire he could so easily ignite in her. "You're attracted to me," she blurted.

"You're a good-looking woman," he replied. His jaw firmed even more. "But you don't have to worry. I gave you my word this would be a marriage in name only. I'll keep my distance."

She watched in stunned silence as he again stalked out of the room.

Absently she forked another bite of wedding cake into her mouth. The idea that had been nagging at her ever since she'd agreed to this marriage returned full force. All they had between them was lust. But that wasn't such a bad position to be in, she reasoned. Both knew this marriage wouldn't last. They had no expectations to be dashed. When they parted there would be no hurt. The sense of adventure returned.

Her legs felt a little wobbly as she left the kitchen. "Nothing ventured, nothing gained," she murmured under her breath. "All work and no play makes Jane a dull girl. Out of the frying pan and into the fire." Frowning at herself, she discarded this last adage.

Stopping outside Sam's door, she gave it one sharp rap, then tried the knob. It was unlocked. Opening the door, she entered as he flipped on the light.

Lying propped up on an elbow, he scowled at her. "What's the problem now?"

"Sleeping alone is not how I pictured my wedding night," she said bluntly.

His gaze narrowed on her. "You and I both know this marriage doesn't have a chance of lasting."

"I didn't say I was interested in forever," she returned, letting him know she had no intention of permanently stripping him of his freedom. As she spoke, she moved toward the bed. Her heart pounded in her chest. She'd never behaved so boldly before.

"Are you sure you know what you're doing?" he asked gruffly, continuing to watch her guardedly.

Sarah's jaw firmed with purpose. "I've been waiting a lot of years for Mr. Right to come along. He never has. If I wait any longer I may never find out what all the shouting is about."

Surprise replaced his guardedness. "Are you saying you've never been with a man?"

"Never," she admitted glumly. Nervousness caused a sudden mischievous grin to play at the corners of her mouth. "This is your chance to be a real hero. And you won't have to worry about me comparing you to anyone else."

Heat blazed in the dark depths of his eyes. "I wasn't looking forward to all the cold showers I figured I'd be taking," he admitted huskily. Lifting the blanket, he invited her to join him.

As she tossed her robe on the chair with his jeans and shirt, then slipped her feet out of her slippers, Sarah's heart beat so hard against her chest it was painful. She had never been this nervous in her life.

I could be really disappointed, she warned herself as she slipped in under the covers. But as he drew her into his arms and she felt the hard musculature of his chest beneath her palms, a fire ignited within. Then his lips found hers. There was a hunger in his kiss that matched her own. Excitement swept through her as she entered a whole new world of physical sensations.

And this *is* something to shout about, she thought as his hands traveled along the curves of her body, awakening a passion that shocked her by its intensity. Feeling almost frantic for even more intimate contact, she helped him discard her nightgown.

"Not too fast," he cautioned gruffly, and she wondered if he was talking to her or himself. It didn't matter, she decided as he trailed kisses downward along her neck and tendrils of fire spread through her.

"Not too slow, either," she murmured back.

"No, not too slow, either," he promised.

She thought she was going to shriek from sheer ecstasy when he tasted her shoulders then slowly worked his way to the hollow of her neck. As if guided by some primitive instinct she had not even known she possessed, she raked her fingernails along his back and her body arched toward his, begging for a more complete union.

He teased her hardened nipples with his tongue and her blood raced. In spite of the confidence in her manner when she'd climbed into his bed, a small nagging worry that she might suddenly become embarrassed or decide this was a bad decision had persisted at the back of her mind. Now, as his touch became more intimate, delight permeated every fiber of her being. This was exactly where she wanted to be, she proclaimed silently, those worries vanishing completely. Then he shifted his body and her breath locked in her lungs. She knew he was preparing to claim her.

Aware that the first time could be painful, she braced herself and vowed not to pass judgment on this first experience. But he was unexpectedly considerate. A momentary discomfort caused her to stiffen. Pausing, he gently caressed her until her body began to relax. Then moving to an age-old rhythm, he again roused her passion until she was lost in a whirlpool of delicious sensation.

* * *

"That," she said, a little later as her breathing returned to normal, "was fun."

"I'm glad you enjoyed it. I did," he replied, giving her seat a final little playful pat, then releasing her and turning onto his back.

Scooting away just enough so that she, too, could lie on her back. Sarah grinned up at the ceiling. Her marriage to Sam had met all her expectations and then some. Well, the past few minutes had anyway.

A lazy satiety spread through her until every fiber of her being felt lulled into relaxation. Contentment blanketed her.

"Maybe now we can get some sleep," Sam said gruffly, reaching to switch off the light.

His body brushed against her and to her surprise desire once again sparked to life within her. Wanton wench! she joked with herself. Still, as he again stretched out beside her and her hand brushed against his thigh, the fire within her grew stronger. "I've heard," she said, "that the second time can be even better than the first."

She felt the bed shift and, in the dark, vaguely made out his silhouette as he levered himself on an elbow to look down at her. "I suppose that could be worth testing."

She heard the question in his voice and knew he was wondering if she was talking about now or sometime in the future. "Now seems like as good a time as any," she answered the silent query.

"Now would be a very good time," he agreed huskily, running his hand along the curve of her hips as his mouth sought hers.

Very good indeed, Sarah thought, happily giving herself up once again to the world of physical pleasure.

Sarah awoke the next morning starving and feeling very pleased with her decision to participate in this marriage. Then she realized she was alone. Frowning at Sam's vacant pillow, she wondered if he was regretting last night. Maybe he was worried about getting trapped in a more personal relationship than he felt comfortable with. Or maybe he was worried that, because they'd actually consummated the marriage, she would insist on trying to make their marriage work.

The thought that she wouldn't mind sharing his bed for a lifetime crossed her mind. Immediately she scowled at herself. Admittedly she and Sam had been able to maintain a reasonably stable truce for better than two weeks now but that was because they knew it was only temporary. As she showered and dressed, she promised herself that at the first opportunity, she'd again assure him she had no intention of shackling him for life.

A little later she was in the kitchen eating a plate of scrambled eggs when she heard him kicking off his boots on the back porch.

"Hope I didn't wake you," he said as he entered and stripped off his gloves. "I knew if I didn't get out there and get the chores done, Orville would be trying to do everything himself in spite of his arthritis." He'd discarded his coat as he spoke. Hanging it on a peg, he added, "Soon as I wash up, I'll join you." Before Sarah could say anything, he was on his way out of the kitchen.

She frowned at his departing back. She'd seen the uneasiness on his face. Obviously she'd guessed correctly. He was worried she might insist on trying to make the marriage work. A curl of rejection twisted through her. That's not fair, she cautioned herself. The two of you never agreed to any kind of personal commitment. In fact, you did just the opposite. This is, for all practical purposes, nothing more than a business arrangement. Still, the sting remained.

When he returned a few minutes later she was braced to tell him coolly that she had no intention of hog-tying him. But before she could open her mouth, he said, "I want to thank you for last night."

"You're welcome," she replied automatically. Then noting that his uneasiness had grown, she continued coolly, "If you're worried that the loss of my virginity has made me feel that we should be bound together for life, you can put your mind at ease. As far as I'm concerned, this marriage is still strictly temporary."

"I figured that," he replied in an easy drawl. "I've always known that whatever you're looking for, it isn't here." His jaw suddenly tensed with purpose. "But for as long as you are here, I was wondering if you'd like to move into my bed. The nights here can be cold and long. I'd enjoy having your company."

The rejection she'd been feeling vanished. "I'd like having someone to keep me warm on a cold night," she admitted with a crooked grin.

Sam visibly relaxed and his uneasiness disappeared.

He'd been worried she might refuse and he'd be embarrassed, she realized. With that knowledge came another revelation . . . Sam Raven was not as indifferent to the way others felt about him as he liked for people to believe.

Nodding in acknowledgment of her acceptance of his offer, Sam went to the refrigerator and took out a carton of eggs.

"I'll fix your breakfast," she said, rising quickly. Startled by how much she wanted to wait on him, she added with a sheepish grin, "I wouldn't want your energy level to go down too far."

A heat darkened the brown of his eyes as he grinned back and Sarah's heart again seemed to lurch. What we have is merely physical. I am not getting emotionally involved, she assured herself as she began fixing his meal. But she had to confess the strength of her attraction was incredibly strong. I'm just like a kid with a new toy, she reasoned as she cooked his eggs. Once the newness has worn off, my interest will wane.

# *Chapter Nine*

Around four weeks later, Sarah stood looking out the kitchen window toward the barns. It was only midafternoon but outside it looked like dusk and was getting darker by the moment. An inch of fresh snow had fallen in the past half hour and now it was falling faster. Sam had found a break in the fence that morning. He'd repaired it, then ridden out to see if he could spot any strays.

He hadn't taken the walkie-talkie. There had only been a couple of sets of tracks and he was sure the cattle that had gotten out hadn't gone far.

"Where is he?" she seethed under her breath, attempting to mask her growing panic with anger. The attempt wasn't working. Her stomach knotted tighter with fear.

She paced across the room, then back to the window. "I'm going to give him one very large piece of my mind when he gets back," she vowed. "And, in the future, he's not going twenty feet from this house without a walkie-talkie!"

Her gaze shifted to the main house. It was dark and empty. Ruth and Orville were in Arizona. She recalled a week after the wedding, when Orville had come over one afternoon to see Sam.

"Now that you're an official member of the Perry clan, are you still interested in buying this ranch?" he'd asked.

"I am," Sam had answered.

Orville nodded with satisfaction. "Since you and Sarah are so worried about me being here on my own that you've refused to go off on a honeymoon, Ruth and I'll be heading out to Arizona in a couple of days. If we find a place, I'll sell you this ranch." He placed an arm around Sam's shoulders. "I'll be relieved to see this place going to someone who loves it as much as my father did. He'll be glad, too. I've often thought he's probably tossing and turning in his grave, angry with himself for placing that restriction on me."

"I'm glad you feel that way," Sam replied.

Sarah saw the relief on his face and realized he'd been feeling, at least, a little guilty about his ploy to skirt old Jason Perry's wishes.

That afternoon, she baked him a white cake with chocolate icing to celebrate. He'd been surprised that she'd remembered that was his favorite.

"I learned to separate eggs, helping my grandmother bake this kind of cake for you," she'd explained.

"I guess I'm lucky other people were going to eat it, too, or there's no telling what I might have found inside," he'd tossed back, reminding her of their embattled adolescence.

That had stirred up an old memory and she'd frowned at him. "I did come very close to throwing in some jalapeño peppers once."

"Just once?" he bantered.

She rewarded him with a dry look, then continued, "It was after I'd been trying to train a horse. He'd gotten squirrelish and started rearing. You grabbed me and dragged me out of the corral, then scolded me in front of several of the wranglers."

His expression became serious. "You nearly got yourself killed or, at the very least, seriously injured that time."

"I suppose," she conceded.

He regarded her narrowly. "Are you sure you're all right? You actually admitted to behaving foolishly."

She tossed him a haughty glance. "I've matured enough to admit the error of my ways." Challenge flickered in her eyes. "The question is, have you matured enough to admit you don't know everything?"

"Every day, life becomes more of a puzzle to me," he replied. Suddenly he grinned playfully. "For instance, what did you put in those biscuits this morning?"

"Nothing that wasn't healthy," she replied.

Unexpectedly he put his arms around her. "Thank you, Sarah," he said and kissed her lightly on the tip of her nose.

She'd been thanked many times by people she'd helped, but she'd never experienced such an intensely warm glow of pleasure. "You're very welcome," she managed to get out around the unexpected lump in her throat. And, as usual, his touch had awakened passion. "This marriage has had its bonuses for me as well," she'd admitted.

He'd read the heat in her eyes and an answering fire kindled in his gaze.

Sarah shivered as fear that she would never feel his arms around her again jolted her mind back to the present. If he wasn't back soon, she was going to saddle a horse and go looking for him, she promised herself. Common sense told her this would be foolish but she refused to listen. I will find him, she assured herself.

Unable to stand still, she paced the floor again. "I should insist on hanging a bell around his neck when he leaves the house," she muttered.

The sound of a horse's whinny caught her attention. Dashing to the window, she saw Sam riding into the barn. Relief swept through her, then came a surge of fury for the fear he'd put her through.

But in spite of her anger, she watched the barn, impatient for another glimpse of him. For practical reasons, I want to make certain he's truly all right, she told herself. After all, it was only the two of them there to run the ranch and, although she knew a little about ranching, she wasn't confident about running the place on her own. Then she saw him come out of the barn and head for the house. He looked uninjured.

Immediately she went over to the stove and began stirring the chili she had simmering there. Just be nonchalant, she ordered herself. As he entered, she merely glanced at him out of the corner of her eye, then forced her attention back to the chili.

"It's getting nasty out there," he said, hanging up his coat.

As if I hadn't noticed, she thought sarcastically. Just agree and keep cool, she ordered herself. But the panic she'd been feeling for the past hour bubbled to the surface. "Didn't you see the storm coming?" she demanded icily. Turning to face him, she heard herself adding, "Surely a couple of cattle aren't worth risking your life for."

"I got back before it got really bad," he pointed out.

He looks half-frozen, she thought. Since the sky had darkened and snow started to fall, she'd fought seeing the image of him lying injured, freezing to death. Now that image filled her mind. Her jaw tensed until it felt painfully rigid. "Next time you go farther than the barns, take a walkie-talkie," she ordered.

His gaze narrowed on her. "You're beginning to sound like a wife," he warned.

Just how much she felt like his wife shook her. His gaze had become guarded and she guessed he was suddenly worried she might want to try to make their union permanent. "I simply prefer to leave this marriage as a carefree divorcée rather than in widow's weeds," she declared haughtily and quickly returned her attention to her cooking.

"That sounds more like the Sarah I know," he observed dryly, then strode out of the kitchen and down the hall.

Gathering the ingredients for corn bread, Sarah drew a shaky breath. The words "Mrs. Sam Raven" and "Sam's wife" played through her mind. She'd never really thought of herself in those terms before. Now they taunted her.

"The man would be impossible to live with on a permanent basis," she grumbled under her breath and again forced her full concentration on cooking dinner.

But much later, in the small hours of the morning, she found herself lying in the dark, watching him sleep. She pictured him here alone, running the ranch on his own. Who would know if he was injured or sick and needed help? she wondered. Fear for him pervaded her. He can take care of himself, she told herself.

Pushing her fear aside, she pictured herself repacking her belongings into her truck and driving away. A pain—as if a part of her was being ripped out—tore through her.

Silently she groaned. She'd fallen in love with Sam Raven! I'm not in love, I'm merely infatuated, she corrected herself. After all, he was her first lover and their lovemaking was very enjoyable. Satisfied that she again had her emotions under control, she slept.

A little over a week later, Sarah again stood at her kitchen window watching Sam down by the barn. This time there was a wistful expression on her face.

Yesterday, they'd paid their usual obligatory visit to his grandmother. His father had been there and while John Raven and Sam had visited, White Flower had taken Sarah aside for a private conversation.

"Come," she'd said, her voice more of an order than a request. Rising from her rocking chair, she'd motioned for Sarah to follow her.

Sam had looked away from the conversation he was having with his father. There was a guardedness in his eyes and Sarah was sure he was going to try to prevent White Flower from proceeding with whatever she had in mind. But his father had placed a restraining hand on Sam's arm. Sam hadn't relaxed but he had not interfered.

White Flower led Sarah into her bedroom. Hand-woven blankets lay hung over the backs of the chairs as if waiting to be wrapped around the shoulders of whoever sat down. Indian rugs were scattered on the floor. A large dream catcher, decorated with feathers, stones and other keepsake ornamentation attached to its spider-web-like centre, hung on the wall above the head of the bed. On the other walls were hung what Sarah was sure were medicine shields. Wooden carvings and handmade dolls covered nearly every inch of the surface of the table in front of the window as well as the one beside the bed and the dresser.

Sarah had never liked clutter and this room could only be described as cluttered. But in this instance, she felt totally at ease. It was as if the room itself exuded a sense of well-being.

White Flower motioned for her to shut the door. When she had complied, the old woman smiled a conspiratorial smile. "I have been preparing something for you," she said.

Sarah was still not certain White Flower truly approved of her marriage to Sam. The sudden vision of the wicked queen dressed as a poor beggar woman handing Snow White the poison apple came into her mind. Frowning at herself for this melodramatic thought, she smiled plastically.

White Flower went to the table by the window and picked up a small wooden box. Carrying it back to where Sarah waited, her manner became solemn as she opened it to reveal two stick figures, one dressed as a boy and the other as a girl. "Because you are older, I have taken great pains to be certain these were laid in a place of great power for three nights," the elderly woman said. "You must put this box with the dolls inside under your bed and your children will be born strong and healthy and live many years."

Sarah had accepted the box in the same solemn manner with which it was given. But it was not under her bed as instructed. Children were definitely not a part of her arrangement with Sam.

On her wedding night, she'd been fairly certain she was within the period of her cycle when she could not conceive. Still, she'd noticed that Sam had been more relaxed after there was evidence that there would be no consequences. Also, following the first night they'd spent together, Sam had made certain they'd taken precautions to ensure against pregnancy.

Further proof the box did not belong under her bed came during their ride home from his grandmother's. Noticing the box, Sam had asked, "Is that what my grandmother wanted to give you?"

Sarah had made up her mind to fabricate a story about the purpose of the gift rather than tell him the real truth. She was certain it would make him uncomfortable. But, instead, she heard herself saying, "It's supposed to ensure that we have strong, healthy children." What really surprised her was how interested she was in his response.

As she'd expected, he stiffened. "I'm sorry you had to be subjected to another of her traditions." Apology mingled with annoyance in his voice.

"I didn't mind," she replied honestly, congratulating herself for having guessed right about what his reaction would be.

And so, the box had taken its place beside the necklace White Flower had given her on her wedding day. And it, too, would be left with Sam when she departed.

Her mind returning to the view beyond the window, Sarah sighed heavily. The thought of having children had not seriously crossed her mind in years. Now as she watched Sam, she found herself picturing a miniature of him trotting along beside him. And a little girl in the kitchen with her, she added.

"This marriage isn't going to last long enough for me to even go through a pregnancy. Besides, Sam isn't interested in me having his child," she reminded herself. This last acknowledgment brought a sharp jab of pain.

Sarah's chin trembled as she finally faced the truth. She wanted to be the forever kind of wife to Sam. She wanted to bear his children. "I have fallen in love with him," she groaned under her breath.

Barely two weeks later, the phone rang as Sarah and Sam were sitting down to supper. It was Orville.

"He and Ruth have found a place in Arizona near where Ruth's sister lives," Sam informed her a few minutes later as he joined her at the table.

Sarah experienced a sinking feeling in the pit of her stomach. Outwardly she forced a smile. "Congratulations. Looks like your plan worked perfectly."

Sam nodded. "It'll take a while for all the paperwork on both places to be processed and for Ruth and Orville to get moved. But then the ranch will be mine."

And as soon as it is, I'll be welcome to pack my bags and leave, Sarah finished silently. She'd finally found her Mr. Right but he considered her his Miss Wrong.

Sam had eaten a bite of food but as he started to carry another to his mouth, he paused and looked at her. "Orville will understand you taking off to do some private nursing if I tell him we want extra money to improve the place. But it would be easier to keep up the appearance of this marriage if you were to stick around for a while after the paperwork is completed. Truth is, I'm going to miss you. It's nice to come home to a good meal and I've gotten used to having you here. If you don't have any plans, you're welcome to stay on for as long as you like."

He was asking her to stay! Well, not exactly asking, she corrected. He was offering her the opportunity. And that offer was only being made because he liked a hot meal on his table and a warm body in his bed. Still, that could change. He could learn to care for her, she argued.

As encouragement, she recalled that through the years, he had sought his grandmother's aid to keep her safe. You're grasping at straws, she warned herself. Opportunity knocks but once, came the rebuttal. Aloud she said, "Thanks, I'll think about it. I've sort of gotten used to being here myself."

He nodded in acceptance of her response and returned to his meal.

Sarah experienced a wave of disappointment. Well, you didn't expect him to jump up and shout hallelujah, she chided herself. Still, keeping her hopes alive, she reminded herself that it had taken her a while to admit her real feelings. And winning Sam was certainly worth devoting a little more of her time to.

# Chapter Ten

Sarah stood on the back porch of the main house. A mild breeze, carrying the scent of winter, stirred her hair. It was nearing the end of September. The ranch had become Sam's nearly five months ago.

A child's laughter caught her attention and she glanced toward the foreman's house. Sam had hired Joe Longbow as permanent help. Joe, his wife, Jane, and their two young children now lived in the foreman's house.

Jane was hanging out laundry while her four-year-old played with their toddler. Noticing Sarah looking her way, she waved and Sarah waved back but made no move to join her. Instead Sarah shifted her gaze to the west in the direction Sam had ridden off this morning.

The sounds of the children playing taunted her and a wistful expression came over her face. Lately she'd begun wishing more and more for a child . . . her and Sam's child. She'd kept herself in good shape. Still, she knew she should not wait much longer for motherhood.

Her jaw firmed and she forced herself to face the truth. "It's not going to happen. This marriage isn't going the way I'd hoped." She'd made herself say the words aloud, hoping that would help her accept the truth once and for all. A sharp pain pierced her.

Her mind traveled back over the past months. Sam had been a thoughtful husband and an exciting lover, but he had not fallen in love with her. And, lately, she'd sensed a growing tenseness in him. At first, she tried to tell herself that his edginess was simply due to tiredness. He'd begun implementing some of the changes he wanted to make such as building new corrals and a stable. There was a lot of work to do and that had meant putting in some very long hours.

Her chin threatened to tremble. Lately those long hours were much longer than necessary, she confessed. And the other night after they'd made love, when he'd thought she was asleep, she'd seen him standing at the window looking out. His stance had been rigid and although she'd had only moonlight to discern his features, she'd been certain there was a troubled expression on his face.

She'd considered letting him know she was awake and asking if she could help solve whatever problem was bothering him. But she hadn't. She'd been too afraid of what he might say.

"He's getting tired of having me here," she said, speaking aloud the thought that had been nagging at her since that night. She told herself she should go inside and pack. Instead she headed for the corral to saddle her horse.

It was turning to dusk when Sarah returned to the ranch. She hadn't been thinking about how far she'd ridden until she realized how late it was getting. Then she'd had to run her horse to get home before dark. As she reached the barn and dismounted, she saw Sam striding toward her.

"Where the hell have you been?" he demanded in a low growl as he reached her.

He looked more angry than concerned, she thought. Still, she felt guilty about worrying him. "I went for a ride," she tossed back over her shoulder as she led her horse into the barn. Remembering one of the main reasons she was still at the ranch, she added stiffly, "Sorry dinner wasn't on the table waiting for you."

His hand closed like a vise around her arm and he jerked her to a halt. "I don't give a damn about dinner! You should have told Jane where you were going. Don't you realize how much worry you caused everyone? I was getting ready to form a search party."

The angry reprimand in his voice made her feel like a nuisance he was being forced to put up with. She pulled free from his hold. "I'm sorry about worrying anyone. I was saying goodbye to the land. I've decided it's time for me to be moving on." In the face of his anger, she'd expected to feel a sense of relief now that she'd announced her departure. Instead hurt mingled with regret.

Returning her attention to her horse, she began unsaddling the mare. A prickling on the back of her neck let her know Sam was still there. But he remained silent as she pulled the saddle off and carried it to its rack. When she started back to her horse, she saw the aloof, stoic expression she'd grown so used to as a girl etched into his features.

"I figured that was coming," he said abruptly, then turned and walked away.

She fought back hot tears of frustration as she brushed down her mare. Fool! Fool! Fool! she chided herself, admitting that she'd hoped he would try to dissuade her. You saw the writing on the wall, she admonished herself.

When she entered the kitchen a few minutes later, she discovered coffee brewing and Sam making a salad. The platter of cold fried chicken left over from the day before was on the table. One place setting had been laid out in front of her chair. A tray sat on the counter.

"I've got some paperwork I need to do," he said. "I'm going to take my dinner into the study."

She merely nodded in acknowledgment and continued on through the kitchen to the bathroom. When she returned a few minutes later, he was gone. As she poured herself a cup of coffee, she noted the darkness of the brew. Sam liked his coffee strong and she'd grown to like it that way, too. A hollowness filled her as she seated herself at the table.

She picked up a piece of the chicken and took a bite. It felt like a rock when it hit her stomach. Slowly she surveyed the room, taking in every detail. Then mentally she moved through the rest of the house. She'd helped Sam pick out some new furniture but several of the rooms were still fairly bare. Still, this place felt like a home to her.

She'd moved around a lot during her life. And each time she'd left one place, she'd looked forward to a new adventure in the next. This time, all she felt was a deep sadness.

I'll be fine once I'm gone, she assured herself, and forced down another bite.

The door suddenly opened and she stiffened as Sam entered and strode over to the coffeepot. He poured himself a cup then turned to her. "When are you planning to leave?"

"Tomorrow," she replied, deciding she'd better get away as quickly as possible. Her control felt weak and she didn't want it to slip and allow Sam to guess how she really felt. He'd lived up to his end of the bargain and now it was time for her to live up to hers. Forcing a flippancy into her voice, she added, "Once I make my mind up, I'm all action."

"I've noticed," he said and left.

Sarah's stomach was a knot. Giving up her attempt to eat, she put the remainder of the food away, straightened the kitchen, then went in search of her trunk and suitcases.

She was in the attic, wondering how she was going to get the trunk down the narrow staircase, when Sam joined her. "I was thinking," he said. "You'll need a home base between assignments. You might as well use this place.''

Sarah had to admit she was tempted. Then she found herself already hoping that when she did come back the first time, he'd have missed her so much, he'd ask her to stay for good. But he won't and the hurt will just be worse, she told herself. ''Thanks for the offer, but I don't think that's such a good idea,'' she replied.

For a moment he looked as if he was going to say something else, then he merely gave a shrug of indifference and offered her help getting the trunk downstairs. When they got it to the bedroom, he left her to begin packing and went back up to the attic to get her suitcases.

Alone in the room, Sarah opened a bureau drawer and took out the necklace and box White Flower had given her. Her hands shook as she laid them on top of the dresser to be returned to Sam. You knew this wouldn't last, she reminded herself again sternly. Make your exit with dignity.

Sam entered with the suitcases at that moment. ''You can go ahead and file for divorce. And we don't need to keep up a pretense for Orville,'' he said as he set them down then straightened to face her.

Sarah frowned at him in confusion.

''The day he and I signed the papers on this place, he told me his conscience was clear. Then he said he knew marriages didn't always last but he'd lived up to his promise to his father and that was all that mattered. He left it at that, but it's my guess he'd figured out what we were up to and was telling me he was willing to go along with it," Sam finished, then strode out of the room.

Sarah stood frozen, listening to his departing boot steps. Don't get your hopes up, she warned herself, but already her legs were carrying her out the door and down the hall. She caught up with him in the kitchen. "I thought the whole reason for you putting up with me being here this long was to keep up the act for Orville's sake."

A flicker of self-consciousness showed from behind his impassive mask. "I liked having you around. I figured your wanderlust would surface sooner or later but I didn't see any reason to send you rushing off."

Hurt swept through her. She'd hoped for more. I warned you not to, her inner voice chided. "You just enjoyed having a hot meal and a warm body," she growled, forcing herself to face the cold truth. "And lately you've been getting tired of me." There, she'd said it aloud; that made it official and she could put him out of her mind.

"I can cook my own food and I've never thought of you as just a warm body in my bed," he returned curtly. "And I wasn't the one who was getting tired of our arrangement."

Cynical disbelief showed on her face. "I've seen you growing more and more tense over the past few weeks."

"Because you were getting edgy and I knew you were getting ready to leave."

Hope again grew within Sarah. "I have been edgy," she admitted. "But it wasn't because of any wanderlust." It's time to go for all or nothing, she told herself. Drawing a shaky breath, she continued stiffly, "I've learned to care for you...a lot. Truth is, I've fallen in love with you." An embarrassed flush reddened her cheeks. "I've even been thinking about having your child." Fear that she'd been too open curled through her. Then he smiled.

"I'd hoped if you stuck around long enough, you'd begin to feel that way, but I never really thought it would happen," he confessed gruffly. A tenderness came over his features. "I have always loved you, Sarah. But I've fought it. If I had been called as a shaman, I could not have given you the life you deserved. And there was Ward Anders offering you everything any woman could want." He scowled. "Then after you broke up with Ward and chose a career in the navy, I realized you had a wanderer's blood. I told myself I was smart not to have pursued you. I wanted a wife who would stay by my side. But I could never put you totally out of my mind."

Sarah moved toward him. "My wanderings have all been because I was searching for the place where I belonged."

Sam drew her into his arms. "This is where you belong."

"It certainly feels like the right place," she agreed as his mouth found hers.

Joy flowed through Sarah. She wanted to laugh and cry at the same moment. Never had his kiss tasted so good.

Lifting his head from hers, Sam grinned down at her. "I've told you the logical reasons why I refused to marry May. But there was one other, not so logical, I didn't mention."

Continuing to remain in the safe haven of his arms, Sarah asked, "And what was that?"

"When I told my grandmother that I did not wish to marry May, she insisted that I go on a life quest before I broke the engagement."

Sarah frowned questioningly. "A life quest?"

He kissed the tip of her nose. "It's a seeking of advice or guidance from the Great Spirit."

"Like a religious retreat where one communes with God and discovers their inner self?" she asked.

"I suppose that's as good an analogy as any." He grimaced as if recalling an experience that had not been entirely pleasant. "A life quest requires physical and mental purification before you can begin and my grandmother was very exacting in that department. I fasted for three days and spent more time in a sweat lodge than I care to remember. Then she ordered me to hike to a specifically designated place in the mountains and stay there for three days and nights. All I was to have to eat during that time was water, a bread she had prepared and any berries I found. But I figured it was a small price to pay to stay on her good side."

"A small price," Sarah agreed, thinking that she would not want to be on White Flower's bad side.

His expression became serious. "It was a very frustrating experience. Every night I dreamed about you. One morning I even awoke and, for a brief moment, thought I saw you sitting across the clearing staring at me. I told myself I was reacting to the deprivation. And there was the herbal bread my grandmother had sent along. It reminded me of the bread you and Morning Dove used to concoct. I figured the taste might be activating old memories and that would explain why you were weighing so heavily on my mind.''

Sarah frowned thoughtfully. ''I suppose White Flower wasn't too pleased with my appearance during your quest.''

He grinned sheepishly. ''I never told her about you. I made up a story about me roaming the mountains and plains alone.'' Sarah saw a flicker of pain in his eyes. ''I figured that if you were supposed to be my mate, then I would be living my life alone. I was certain you were deeply in love with Anders and had fled here because of a broken heart.''

''Instead I was searching the world for Mr. Right when I should have been looking in my own backyard,'' she murmured. She kissed him lightly, then asked, ''Were there any children in your visions?''

''Two, I think.'' He drew her closer. ''Mostly you seemed to fill my mind.''

Sarah grinned. ''Clearly we need to begin working on fulfilling your fate.''

''Now seems like as good a time as any,'' he said, slipping his arm around her waist and guiding her out of the kitchen and down the hall.

Happiness swept through her. As they entered their bedroom she wiggled away from him. ''There is just one little thing I want to take care of,'' she said, smiling up at the confusion on his face.

Going to the dresser, she picked up the small box containing the stick figures, carried it to the bed and slipped it underneath.

He grinned, his eyes darkening with purpose.

"And now we shall face our fates together," Sarah said, returning to him and beginning to unfasten his shirt.

# Epilogue

Sarah stood at the second-floor window looking out. It was late August...one month shy of a year since Sam had told her he loved her. From her vantage point, she could see Sam, his father and Orville down by the new corral looking over the breeding stallion Sam had recently purchased.

"Orville's real impressed with what you and Sam have done with this place," Ruth said.

The smile on Sarah's face warmed even more as she turned and her gaze surveyed the room in which she stood. What had once been a guest bedroom was now a nursery. Ruth was seated in one of the two rocking chairs, cradling the newly arrived Molly Raven in her arms. Seated in the second rocking chair was White Feather holding Jason Raven, her newly arrived great-grandson.

"Sam's worked hard," Sarah replied. "But he loves this place, so it has been a labor of love."

"You have made my grandson a happy man," White Feather spoke up. "And blessed our family with these two fine, healthy children."

"I'm the one who feels blessed," Sarah assured her. As the two older women again turned their full attention to the twin babies they were holding, Sarah turned back to the window. Very blessed, she thought watching Sam. Even from this distance, just the sight of him stirred a passion within her.

She recalled the concern on his face when she'd been in labor. And then the pride and love when their twins had been born. The very stoic, aloof Sam Raven existed no more for her. She knew the man beneath the taciturn exterior. He was warm, passionate and caring... the husband, partner and friend she'd been looking for all her life.

As if he sensed her watching him, he looked toward the nursery window. She saw him smile and smiled back.

\* \* \* \* \*

Get Ready to be Swept Away by
Silhouette's Spring Collection

# Abduction
# *& Seduction*

These passion-filled stories explore both the dangerous
desires of men and the seductive powers of women.
Written by three of our most celebrated authors, they are
sure to capture your hearts.

### Diana Palmer
Brings us a spin-off of her Long, Tall Texans series

### Joan Johnston
Crafts a beguiling Western romance

### Rebecca Brandewyne
*New York Times* bestselling author
makes a smashing contemporary debut

Available in March at your favorite retail outlet.

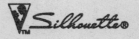

## MILLION DOLLAR SWEEPSTAKES (III)

## SILHOUETTE®
## Desire®

**is**

### DIANA PALMER'S
### THAT BURKE MAN

He's rugged, lean and determined. He's a
Long, Tall Texan. His name is Burke, and he's
March's *Man of the Month*—Silhouette Desire's
75th!

Meet this sexy cowboy in Diana Palmer's
THAT BURKE MAN, available in March 1995!

*Man of the Month*...only from Silhouette Desire!

DP75MOM

If you are looking for more titles by

## ELIZABETH AUGUST

Don't miss this chance to order additional stories by
one of Silhouette's great authors:

### Silhouette Romance™

Silhouette®